The Dying Time

The Dying Time

Bernard Schopen

BAOBAB PRESS
RENO, NV

First Printing

ISBN-13: 978-1-936097-22-7
ISBN-10: 1-936097-22

Library of Congress Control Number:
2018950303

Baobab Press
121 California Avenue
Reno, Nevada 89509
www.baobabpress.com

In Memory of
Kevin Burnside and Jon Gilbert

ONE

The rising November sun lightened the dawn as I jogged in the foothills of the Sierra. Shadows shortened. Sage and rabbit brush nodded in the chill air. My footfalls thumped, my breathing huffed, my heartbeat regulated the day.

The trails I took sometimes climbed out of narrow canyons to offer a panoramic view of the Truckee Meadows. More than half a century before, a boy tramping these paths, I'd looked out onto swaths of green and brown: fields and orchards, marshes, pastures. The arcs and angles of Reno and Sparks, then two small towns, had seemed unobtrusive, accommodated by the land. Now, between the dark mass of the mountains and the pale brown desert ranges, flashes of sunlight on glass accented the gray of growth—rooftops, parking lots, highways and streets, medical complexes and office buildings and warehouses.

I missed what had been. But things change. Life goes on. Then it doesn't.

I jogged, worked up a sweat, and enjoyed the morning until finally my body began to protest. I was an old man, bone and sinew insisted, and it was time I acted my age. I obeyed, turned down Evans Canyon, shuffled into Rancho San Rafael Park, and, after stretching, walked back to my house on a Coleman Street corner.

A while later, fed, showered, and clad in jeans and a University of Nevada, Reno sweatshirt, I set about one more Monday. I started a load of laundry, then sat at my computer in the bedroom I used as an office, working through communications that had collected over the week I'd just spent in the desert. There wasn't much.

My daughter, Cynthia, had emailed a photograph of my granddaughter in her soccer uniform, along with confirmation of plans for me to spend Thanksgiving in Seattle with her and her family. I returned my thanks and love. A local bureaucrat wanted to speak with me on a confidential matter. I told him I was retired. A woman I'd been able to help years earlier had died, and her son thought I'd want to know. I thanked him for his consideration and offered my condolences. The UNR School of the Arts announced the schedule of chamber music concerts by a trio of talented professors. I signed up for the series. I paid a couple of bills and rid my in-box of enticements and solicitations. My paper mail was junk. I had no phone messages.

At midmorning, laundry done, I went out. In the brief driveway, beneath the spread of bare branches of a huge mulberry tree, sat my beat-up Subaru Forester. I backed it out and drove down to a West Fourth Street station, where I filled the gas tank and, in the car wash, scrubbed off the desert grime. Then the routine into which my life had reduced took me to and across the slow-flowing Truckee River into a neighborhood off Mayberry. Once the area had been agricultural: truck gardens, pastures, orchards. A scatter of old fruit trees remained, one in the back yard of a late 60s ranch-style home of well-cared-for brick and plaster.

Today, a pale green BMW was parked before the closed, double-wide garage. I pulled in beside it, then sat a moment. When I was calm, composed, ready to resist old impulses, I got out and went to the door.

Frank Calvetti answered my ring. "Promise to play nice?"

Without allowing me a reply, he turned and shuffled toward the back of the house, his stoop and scuff those of a man elderly and ailing. Frank was my age and struggling with complications from diabetes—cardiac concerns, especially, as well as respiratory and circulatory difficulties—but he'd grown old, not so much through an accumulation of years or afflictions of the flesh, but from attending to Sheila, his wife of a half-century, as she suffered and died of ovarian cancer.

In Sheila's last drug-dazed weeks, I'd sat with him, drinking coffee and advancing pegs around a cribbage board. Some years before that, when Vietnam caught up with me, Frank had sat with me while for six months I wept.

He led me to the large bright kitchen and breakfast nook. At a table, taking tea from a china pot, sat an attractive woman of a certain age. Frank's sister. My ex-wife.

I offered her a careful smile. "Good morning, Alicia."

"Jack."

It was less a greeting than a prickly acceptance of my presence. Her dark hair stylishly streaked, her makeup smoothly subdued, her still slim body clad in dark slacks and a rust-colored sweater, she glared at me.

Alicia too had lost her spouse, when three years earlier Randal Barnes had suffered a massive coronary. Like her brother, she still grieved, but while he often took on the stunned expression of one mortally stricken, she more commonly slipped into the wary, injured anger of the betrayed. She was angry now, with me. This was not unusual.

For some years after I'd fled our marriage, both Alicia and I had said and done things that the other, now, although inclined to forgive, could not forget. Even after fifty years. We had done injury to one another. After our daughter was grown and gone, and our contact was less frequent—we sometimes went several years without meeting—resentment remained.

She spoke then, but not to me. "This won't work, Frank. I still think you should do it."

"Let him see it," her brother said.

Out the kitchen door was a brick patio, beyond which grew a greens garden now bedded beneath a layer of hay and watched over by a small, black-clad scarecrow doll. At the back of the lot stood an old, oft-pruned, now leafless apple tree and a younger plum tree picked of the yellow drupe from which Frank made a potent wine. Alicia, troubled, gazed silently at the scene. Then with a wave of her hand she unhappily directed me to a chair.

From the bag on the table she took an envelope. She held it out to me. "Frank thinks you can help with this."

The remark carried the snap of old antagonism. Or maybe I was imagining. I let it pass, accepted and from long habit studied the envelope.

The paper was heavy, the handwriting small and neat, the local postmark dated a week before. The envelope had been mailed to Mrs. Randal Barnes at Alicia's Caughlin Ranch home. The return address was that of one Mia Dunn, at an apartment on a Reno street I didn't know.

I opened the envelope and removed a business card with work and cell numbers. With it was a note: the same good paper, the same careful hand.

Dear Mrs. Barnes,

I'm trying to identify my father. I think he might have been Randal Barnes. I have materials I'd like to show you, to confirm it.

I don't want to trouble you or make any claims.

I work staggered shifts at Renown South Meadows Medical Center, but you can get my cell machine anytime.

Please help me.

Mia Dunn

"I don't do this anymore," I said hastily. "My license to conduct investigations on behalf of another party lapsed years ago."

"This isn't 'on behalf of another party,'" Frank said with something of his old asperity. "It's family."

Alicia was again staring out at the toy scarecrow and the garden and the fruit trees, as if to separate herself from the note and what it seemed to mean. I thought I understood why she was upset. She didn't want me mucking around in her husband's sex life.

Over the last three years, after decades of disaffection, Alicia and I had managed in our few family encounters not to bellows banked feelings into flame. Our rapprochement, such as it was, had begun at Randal Barnes's funeral. I'd known Randy since high school, we'd started law school together, and we remained cordial after he married Alicia. He was a good guy, steady and solid, quiet, even a bit shy, and ever ready to lend assistance. He loved Alicia wholeheartedly, which for some reason made me like him even more. We had a professional relationship as well. I consulted him when cases raised money questions I couldn't answer; he called me if his business required a certain sort of information. He had helped me upon my return from Vietnam, setting up a trust for my daughter, and giving me investment advice that had produced my present financial security. I'd liked him and owed him, and I mourned his passing. At the service, when I told his widow so, Alicia accepted my sympathies with a sad smile free of enmity. Some months later, our Christmas visits with our daughter and her family overlapped, and, thrown together, we subtly realigned: we conducted ourselves carefully, were civil and circumspect. We were, as grandparents, if not a couple nevertheless something more than acquaintances. We behaved in a friendly manner even though we could never actually be friends.

Our relationship was still—would probably always be—strained. But I didn't want to jeopardize what little progress we'd made by involving myself in her private affairs.

I retreated into legalities. "You have no obligation to this young woman, Alicia, whoever her father might be. But if you want it looked into it, I can recommend a couple of agencies."

"No, thank you." She snapped, waving a dismissive hand. "They'll start talk. They'll interrogate our friends, ask questions, make sleazy insinuations."

Her scowl made clear whom she was accusing.

Resentment roughened my voice. "They'll do what you hire them to do. They'll be discreet. They're professionals."

"Some profession!" She shook her head angrily. "Digging up old secrets and mistakes and betrayals. And how discreet could they be, asking people—people important to me—about my husband fathering a child out of wedlock!"

I teetered on the edge of unpleasantness.

Alicia glared at me again. "I won't let this ruin his reputation. Or mine."

Alicia had for years served on committees and boards, raised money for charities and scholarships and grants, nibbled canapés and sipped cocktails for fashionable causes. She got her name in the paper, once in a while her picture. If she hadn't reached the upper stratum of Truckee Meadows society, it wasn't for lack of trying. If she wasn't quite a pillar of the community, she was certainly a weight-bearing post. She had done much good.

But what she had done was not what she cared about.

"Your reputation." I regretted the words even as they came out of my mouth.

Alicia smiled archly, as if in triumph. "I know you think I'm a superficial person."

"No, look, I'm sorry," I said. "I didn't mean—"

"Of course you did! You always—"

"Give it a rest!" Frank set his teacup onto the saucer with a sharp clack, disgusted.

We fell silent, she stiff with umbrage, I warm with shame. After nearly fifty years, we two were like adolescents, sneering, sniping.

Frank took up the teapot and refilled his cup. "The problem is—"

"The problem is," Alicia interrupted angrily, "you want my ex-husband to ask my friends about my late husband's adultery. I won't have Jack, of all people, snooping into Randy's—into our—sex life."

Frank said, wearily, as if we had exhausted him. "Then forget the whole thing."

Alicia sagged in her chair. "I can't."

Frank tried again. "Jack *knew* Randy, Alicia. He's the only one who can check this out without embarrassing you or scandalizing your friends. You must see that."

"No," she said. "I mean I see, yes, but—"

"Show him," Frank said sternly. "Or let it go."

She looked out at the fruit trees, the garden, the funereal little scarecrow. Then, abruptly, from her bag she withdrew a photograph. "This was with the note."

Two women and two men sat in a curved, padded booth. The women were costumed in tassels and cleavage and meretricious makeup. A plumpish blonde wearing cat's-eye spectacles smiled stiffly beside a good-looking man of thirty or so whom I couldn't quite place. The woman on his other side frowned at the camera as if daring it to deny her worth. Her auburn hair fell nearly to her bare shoulders, which were then encircled by the arm of Randy Barnes. His grin changed his face, made it boyish, eager. His gaze was slightly askew, as if blurred by booze or drugs or lust.

"This looks to be at least twenty-five years ago, at the Blue Flame," Frank said. "The doxies are the sort that Harvey Prior ran."

The Blue Flame had been a downtown topless joint, Harvey Prior a player of consequence in local crime. He reputedly brokered various illegal enterprises, for a fee put together those who wanted with those who had or could get. He ran a car-theft ring, fenced stolen goods, and hired out leg-breakers, and he had muscled his way into a small piece of the local cocaine action. He directed all this from behind the sexual shenanigans that took place in his Lake Street club. He was said to have a collection of photographs, tapes, IOUs, and assorted documents that allowed him to operate with impunity.

"I know about that place," Alicia interrupted again. "Randy did some work for Bryce Ragatz, saved him a lot of money, and Bryce recommended him to the Prior creature. I never understood how Bryce could associate with someone like that." She shook her head, as if to deny reality. "Prior made Randy meet him there, at the club, had his women saunter around half naked while Randy was trying to talk trusts and IRAs. Randy told me all about it, told me everything. At least I thought so. But he didn't tell me about . . . her."

The woman with the auburn hair, she meant. The woman who, alone in the photograph, was unsmiling. The woman who seemed to demand acknowledgement of her value.

"Maybe there was nothing to tell," I said. "These shots are standard in this kind of place, like tourists getting photographed with Vegas showgirls. Maybe he's not with her, maybe—"

"Don't treat me like a simpleton, Jack," she spat. "Of course he's with her! Look at him! Look!"

I saw what she meant, the embrace, the grin. I saw too what she felt.

As if she couldn't abide my awareness of her distress, she rose and jerked open the glass door, sliding it shut behind her as she fled onto the patio.

Frank and I sat silent. Then I said, "What are you up to with all this?"

Because the notion that I was necessary to Alicia's reassurance was nonsense.

"We're all tired of tippy-toeing around you two," he said. "It's time to kiss and make up."

I nodded at Alicia, who stood stiffly in a square of pale sunshine, her back to us. "You see how things are. And you want me to tell her if her husband cheated on her."

He scoffed. "What are the chances of that?"

"Remote," I acknowledged. Randy Barnes was one of the most thoroughly married men I'd ever encountered. "But you never know. Besides, she doesn't want me poking around in her marriage, and I don't blame her."

"Such a scrupulous soul, Jack Ross," he deadpanned. "But even though she married you once, my sister's not really an idiot. She knows you're the only one who can appreciate her concerns."

"You could," I said.

He hesitated, then said, "I'm not up to it."

The admission startled me. Frank had never complained about his health, brushing off the concerns of family and friends with droll ironies and gruff assurances. I looked closely at him. He had returned from a recent hospitalization haggard, flesh sagging on the bones of his face, darkness deepening beneath his eyes.

"Are you all right?"

"I'll live," he said dryly. "I just don't have the energy I used to. All I want to do is sit here with my friend Paltry and watch my garden grow."

Paltry was the scarecrow. A granddaughter had fashioned the figure from popsicle sticks and scraps of black cloth, stuck on a now deeply withered crabapple for a head. It reminded me of a line I'd read many years earlier: "An aged man is but a paltry thing / A tattered coat upon a stick. . . ." Frank had laughed when I mentioned it. The name stuck.

I looked out again at Alicia. She stood slightly slumped, beaten down by emotion or huddled against the chill of the day. "I don't do this sort of thing anymore. I haven't for a long time. You know that, Frank."

Years earlier, long before I retired, even before Vietnam found me out, I'd stopped taking cases for individuals. I worked primarily for insurance companies and attorneys, often as much paralegal as private investigator. In dealings with the distraught, I'd kept my distance.

"But you don't really know what sort of thing this is." Frank rose, as if a decision had been made. "Take an hour out of your terrifically busy schedule, Jack. Talk to this Mia Dunn. Find out what she thinks this photo says, and what else she's got."

"Only if Alicia okays it," I said, rising and moving to the door.

As I stepped out onto the patio, Alicia gave me an unhappy glance. I came to stand beside her, near enough to notice the musky scent she wore. We hadn't stood alone together for nearly fifty years.

I smiled. "We have to stop meeting like this."

"You have to turn everything into a joke, don't you," she said bitterly.

"Just maintaining my balance," I said, as much an apology as an explanation. I took a deep breath. "I'll talk to this young woman, Alicia, if you want me to. Or not."

"I don't want you to, but I suppose Frank's right, it's the only way." She hugged herself, as if against the chill. "I know I don't matter to you, but Randy was your friend. Maybe that counts for something."

I let that pass. "I'll do what I can, carefully. I don't want to injure your reputation. Or Randy's. Or this Mia Dunn's, for that matter."

She looked at me, dubious but worn down. "All right, Jack. All right."

"This could involve science," I said. "Do you have anything that technicians might lift Randy's DNA from? Anything he might have sweated into, golf club or tennis racket grips, shoes, hats, that sort of thing?"

She gave her head an almost imperceptible shake. "Everything went to St. Vincent's. I haven't gone through his home office, but it's only papers, old business stuff."

"Maybe you could take a good look. It might not be necessary, the DNA," I said, "but we should try to get some if we can."

"Yes." Then her shoulders squared. "Frank needs something to do. Can you get him to help you? I don't know what that would mean, but . . ."

Felicia loved her big brother. I did too. We who had once shared a life now shared little, but we shared this. This silent recognition seemed to soften, at least for the moment, the autumn air in which we stood, shivering.

"Yes," I said, nodding. "Good idea."

"One other thing, Jack." She met, held my gaze. "Will you promise that you'll tell me the truth, whatever it turns out to be?"

I looked at her. She was thinking about another promise I'd made to her, one I'd broken. Or maybe I was imagining again.

"Yes," I said. "I promise."

TWO

After Alicia left, Frank got out cards and cribbage board while I called Mia Dunn. At her recorded invitation, I gave my name and cell number and told her that I was an attorney who would be happy to meet her, at a time and place of her choosing, to discuss the note she'd sent to Mrs. Barnes.

The voice had been soft and tentative, the auditory equivalent of her small, careful handwriting. She sounded very young.

Frank and I played cards, speaking only to count or peg. He skunked me the first game, I pegged out on him in the second. As I dealt to begin the third, he said, "Alicia never understood Randy's relationship with you. She thought he was being disloyal."

"'Alicia *no capisce.*'" It was the refrain of a Louis Prima song, which many years before a pair of uncertain adolescents cited to express their failure to comprehend the deeds and moods of a girl becoming a woman. "Besides," I added, "she felt the same about you. So did your folks."

After Alicia filed for divorce, her father cursed me and her mother removed me from her prayers. They insisted that Frank end our friendship. He refused, at what cost I had never been certain.

I waited, but he changed the subject, nodding at the photograph that Alicia had left on the table. "The other guy. You don't remember?"

"Seems familiar," I said. Cropped blond hair, even features, tight easy smile, he looked a bit like the actor Steve McQueen, but affable rather than intense. "Can't place him, though."

"You weren't much interested in the news about then," Frank said. "Try Ragatz."

"Ragatz," I repeated, memory stirred. "Bryce's what, cousin? Went missing, decamped, or something?"

"Or something. Howie Ragatz, by name."

Frank dealt a hand, and we played on as he reminded me.

The media had made much of the disappearance of Howie Ragatz. Reporters insisted on identifying the missing man as the nephew of Carl Ragatz, a pioneer in the gaming business in Reno and a philanthropist with deep pockets, whose name appeared on scholarships, streets, and parks. Since his death, his charitable activities had been managed by Carlotta Farragut Ragatz, the daughter of another early casino operator, Denny Farragut, and, as well, the wife of Carl Ragatz's son, Bryce, athlete of local repute, war hero, and casino operator, now retired.

Howie was the offspring of Carl Ragatz's dissolute distant cousin, an Ely bartender/bouncer long dead. Carl had disavowed any important tie, and Bryce, although he had hired and liked Howie, had ignored his efforts to establish familial intimacy. Bryce had, however, put up the cash for his cousin's bail bond.

"Which he skipped out on," Frank said. "They had him for coke possession. He was looking at a stretch in the slam, and word was he wanted no part of prison, so he ran. Then again, some said he lit out from people he'd stiffed in the cocaine business, or he ditched his wife and son and ran off with a bimbo. Smart money said he was dead, killed by suppliers or other dealers in a dope fuss. In any case, he was among the absent. Still is."

I had no interest in Howie Ragatz, unless he turned out to be Mia Dunn's father. But Alicia had wanted Frank involved. "Any chance you could get me the file?"

My contacts in local law-enforcement circles were long departed into death or retirement. Frank, on the other hand, though some years past RPD service, breakfasted regularly with old cronies, and he still knew people who knew people.

He counted his crib and pegged out. "I can ask around."

My phone rang. Mia Dunn. I answered, identified myself, and listened.

She did want to meet. She wanted to talk about Randal Barnes. Her mother had recently passed away, and going through her papers, Mia found letters that suggested Mr. Barnes might be her father.

She spoke hesitantly, phrases rising on an interrogative lilt, not stated so much as ventured, proposed as possibilities.

We agreed to meet in two hours at a coffee shop called Good Beans near the Renown South Meadows Medical Center.

Our games done, Frank and I talked, briefly, about his family, sons and daughters-in-law and several grandchildren. We didn't talk about his sister. We didn't talk about his dead wife. We didn't talk about his health, physical or emotional.

Finally, I left him with Paltry to watch his garden not grow.

I drove home, had a bowl of soup, and watched local TV news anchors flirt and giggle between items: war in the Mideast, search for terrorists in Paris, murder in Chicago, blather from aspirants for president, a mugging in Sparks, a barn fire in Warm Springs.

I exchanged my sweatshirt for a yellow button-down shirt and a blue blazer, looked up the address for Good Beans, grabbed a couple old business cards, and left again.

A late noon rush had the ramps to both I-80 and I-580 backed up. Traffic south was contentious. Then, when I finally reached the exit I wanted, in a moment of uncertainty I turned the wrong way and was immediately lost.

Everything here was new, developments laid over erstwhile pastures and hayfields, T-squared and French-curved streets, acres of homes desperate to be different, mini-malls and franchised businesses: a generic world, Anywhere USA.

The GPS I'd installed in the Forester when I was working was long defunct, and I hadn't thought I'd need a map of my home town. I finally came upon the hospital, went looking for the coffee shop, passed the hospital again, and ended up creeping through a housing development that seemed a wasteland—draped windows and green garbage cans and an occasional car parked before a closed garage. Sheer luck brought me to the street I wanted.

Good Beans occupied a rectangle of cement blocks, which thick coats of coffee-brown paint failed to disguise. I parked next to a newish blue Toyota Yaris in an otherwise empty lot. The coffee house too was nearly empty, dim, not quite warm. A pair of bored baristas offered me half-hearted smiles. Three young men in white shirts and dark ties whom, had they not been drinking coffee, I would have taken for Mormon missionaries, ignored me. The young woman in hospital scrubs at a table in the center of the room did not.

I'd expected small, thin, weak, but although she was not tall, she was big-boned and broad-shouldered. She looked like she should be stacking cartons in a warehouse or wrestling calves in a corral.

"Ms. Dunn?"

She patted nervously at her frizzy reddish hair, even as her timorous voice confirmed her identity: "I, yes . . . Mr. Ross?"

"May I sit down?"

She was not reassured by my smile. I wasn't what she'd expected either—big, old, blue-jeaned. I smiled again and offered her a business card and sat across from her.

"You're a private investigator too?" She seemed alarmed.

"Long retired," I said.

A manila envelope lay on the table beside her coffee cup. She covered it with a protective hand.

I took out the note and photograph. "Mrs. Barnes isn't sure what to make of these. You say your mother had the photo?"

She tugged the envelope farther away from me. "And some letters. She . . ."

Slowly, cautiously, sometimes speaking so softly I had difficulty hearing her, she offered an account of the photos, and of her mother, and of herself.

Mia Dunn was an ER nurse, two years past her UNR graduation. She'd grown up on an alfalfa farm outside Gardnerville. Her grandfather was long dead, her grandmother now a year in a Minden nursing home. Her mother had left home at sixteen, returned when Mia was born, and eventually took over the farm. She'd died two months earlier in a fall from a tractor. She'd been intoxicated.

Gale Dunn had always been a binge drinker, but this last year, living alone, she'd deteriorated, began to lose control, got mean and paranoid. She had a DUI. She was taken in for disturbing the peace. She telephoned people at all hours and said awful things.

Mia Dunn squared her shoulders, as if to meet a challenge. "My grandfather died of a heart attack in his fifties. My grandmother is half blind with glaucoma. My mother had issues with alcohol and emotional instability. So you can see why I'd want to know who my father was. What else might be in my genetic profile?"

"Yes," I said. "And the photograph?"

"I had to go through her papers, looking for insurance forms?" she said. "I found it. And there were letters? They made me think . . . ?"

She paused, looked at me as if for help. I smiled, waited.

The skin around her nose, beneath her eyes, slowly reddened. Her eyes shimmered.

"On my birth certificate, my father is listed as 'unknown.' My mother wouldn't talk about him, she said she didn't know who'd got her pregnant? She'd been an exotic dancer. I was an accident." Her eyes took on a glaze. "I didn't really believe her? How could she not know?"

"If she was sexually . . ." I searched for a decorous word.

"I know what she was." Mia Dunn said, blinking at her tears. "Not a prostitute, really, not like in a brothel. But . . . ?"

This was painful for her. I tried to ease her past it.

"She ran the farm? She must have managed things well, to pay for your education?"

"But I should have known, shouldn't I? That much money? There wasn't any way the farm could have had that kind of profit?"

I was getting the picture. "Why don't you show me what you have that makes you think Randal Barnes might have been your father?"

She pursed her lips uncertainly. She patted at her hair.

Mia Dunn was not pretty, but her green eyes were fine, her features, though heavy, were open, pleasant, clean, her mouth soft, her skin smooth—she seemed innocent still, and in that attractive.

She hesitated, then handed me the envelope. "These are copies."

Inside were three letters, each on the stationary of a local Wells Fargo branch. The gist of the first, dated June of 1990, was that money had been placed in a trust account, from which Gale Dunn would receive each month a check for four hundred dollars, until her daughter, Mia, finished high school, after which time funds would be available to pay for Mia's tuition at any accredited college or university. The second letter congratulated Mia on her graduation from Douglas High School and announced that monthly checks would cease and that requests for tuition to an institution of higher learning should be submitted to the bank. The third, dated two years ago, again congratulated Mia, this time for having earned a nursing degree from UNR. An enclosed check would clear the funds remaining in the account. Once it was cashed, all financial assistance would end.

Each letter was signed by a different bank vice-president. The source of the money was not identified, nor was the original amount in the trust specified.

The second and third letters were addressed to Mia. "You hadn't seen these?"

She shook her head. "My mother . . . she didn't want me to know?"

"And what in all this led you to conclude that Randal Barnes was your father?" But even as I spoke, I saw it.

Someone—the third VP, a secretary?—had made a mistake. At the bottom of the final letter was a note that a copy had been sent to Randal Barnes.

"I didn't conclude, exactly?"

She'd found the letters. She'd found the photograph of the man with his arm around her mother. She'd found a picture with the obituary of Randal Barnes on the internet. She assumed. Guessed. Hoped.

"Randal Barnes handled other people's money, Miss Dunn. That may be what's going on here." I nodded at the photograph. "And that's just a shot of a couple of guys having a good time at a strip club. The way they're all together, well, it's hard to say anybody's with anybody. She could just as easily be with the other guy."

"I didn't know who he is, though?" She said. "Do you?"

I nodded. "Howie Ragatz."

The name meant nothing to her. "Is he . . . could I talk to him?"

"He's not around anymore, hasn't been for years," I said.

Dismay clouded her green eyes. "It's just not knowing? Who am I?"

She seemed again near tears.

"On my birth certificate, the father listed is Virgil Ross, my mother's ex-husband," I said quietly. "But Virgil Ross left town two years before I was born. People knew. They speculated. Men looked at me and snickered. Women for some reason found me a threat. There were homes in Reno where I wasn't welcome. Other kids . . . well, you know what kids do."

She nodded. "Did you ever find out who your father was?"

"No," I said. "Finally I got to the point that it didn't matter."

Mia Dunn hadn't reached that point yet.

We sat in silence. Then I said, "Tell me about your mother. What was she like?"

"She was unhappy?" the young woman said, unhappy herself. "And angry. She was mad at everybody? She thought everybody had, I don't know, cheated her, I guess. Even me. I didn't know why, I worked hard on the place, I got good grades in school, I was nice? I don't know why she didn't love me?"

She was struggling, her voice nearly a whisper. She was as emotionally fragile as she was physically robust. She seemed to be encountering rather than recounting feelings.

"Did she have any close friends? Men? Girlfriends? Anyone she might have talked to about herself."

"No, no men. Even though guys tried, you know? But she blew them off, except a couple of times when she was drinking? She didn't have any friends—especially not at the end, after she started calling people at all hours of the night, saying horrible things." She pointed to the blonde woman wearing cat's-eye spectacles. "That's Tabby Sabich, a friend from her dancing days. She came out to the farm a few times when I was real little. When I found the letters and picture, I searched Google and Twitter and Facebook, but there's no Tabby or Tabitha Sabich listed anywhere."

I smiled. "Maybe I can find her for you."

She brightened. "Oh, could you? I'd really like to talk to her. I mean, she might know. And the other man, Ragatz? Howie? There's no way to contact him?"

"He disappeared years ago." As I spoke, however, I had a thought. "But we might not need him. He had a son. If I could find him, we might get a DNA sample to compare to yours."

"You'd do that?" She didn't try to mask her doubt. "I mean, you work for Mrs. Barnes?"

"I represent her interests, yes," I said. "But if Howie Ragatz was your father, then Randal Barnes wasn't."

Mia Dunn smiled then, a small smile, tentative, testing, but a smile nevertheless.

She had to go to work. I gathered the copies of the three letters, stuffed them in my pocket, and then walked her out to her car, the blue Yaris.

As she opened the door, she turned to me. "You . . . you'll really try? To find out who my father was, I mean?"

"Yes," I said.

She nodded soberly. "My mom. She could be mean, but she was very brave. She had an AVM--an Arteriovenous Malformation. Doctors found it when she got pregnant. She never told anyone. I only learned about it after she died, when I went through her papers."

She seemed surer, more confident when she spoke of medical matters. Now she saw that I didn't know what an AVM was.

"It's a sort of tangle of veins and arteries in the brain. You're born with it. A stroke was inevitable, but there was no way to predict it. At any moment she could have been crippled or killed." She sighed. "She lived with it all those years, with death in her head. And then she got drunk and fell off a tractor."

MY MORNING RUN had taken a lot out of me. I was ready for a nap. But when I got home, I went into my office and laid out on my desk the photograph, letters, and note, hoping I might see something I hadn't seen before.

The note, now that I'd spoken with Mia Dunn, struck me as naïve, poignant. She was a young woman not fully formed.

The letters deliberately hid the particulars of the money. Who had, in effect, paid child support for Mia Dunn? Was it Randy Barnes? I didn't think so. Randy was a kindly, do-gooding sort, but this seemed beyond him. Still, I couldn't be sure.

I concentrated on the photograph. The young blonde, Tabby Sabich, hard-eyed behind her glittery glasses, smirked. Howie Ragatz's small smile said that he was supremely satisfied with himself. Randy Barnes's grin made him young, surprised by sudden possibilities. Gale Dunn glowered. I could find nothing about her face or figure to suggest that she could detach Randy Barnes, a most uxorious man, from his wife.

Gale Dunn was living under the imminent threat of severe injury or death. How might that have affected her? I had lived so for only a year in Vietnam, but I never quite recovered.

I thought again about Alicia and the promise I'd made to her. I thought about Mia Dunn, to whom I'd made a promise as well.

The bed in the next room beckoned. I resisted. I fired up my computer and went to work.

I had years of experience, good instincts, and special software. By the time the day had gone dark, I had names and addresses. I called Mia Dunn, went to voice mail, and told her that Tabitha Sabich lived in the Lemon Tree Apartments, at an address off Rock Boulevard in Sparks. I also told her that the next day I would be speaking to the young man I felt fairly sure was Howie Ragatz's son.

In a locked bottom drawer in my desk I kept important papers, certificates, policies, and financial materials. I kept there too, in an old teak box, my grandfather's .38 Smith and Wesson. Now I placed with it the photo and note I'd gotten from Alicia, the letters from Mia Dunn.

I heated and ate a slab of Raley's lasagna, rinsed and stacked my dishes, poured a couple of inches of Glenlivet over ice, put on a CD of Yo-Yo Ma playing Schubert, and settled into my chair. I sat and sipped as, out the window, the evening dimmed the chilling city.

What had begun as one more unremarkable day in my now unremarkable life had turned into hours of emotional tension. I'd made promises. I'd been troubled by the physical decline of my friend. I'd watched my ex-wife suffer. I'd attended a young woman as she spoke of her loneliness.

I drank my scotch, listened to the music, watched the flicker of city lights and night stars, and, perhaps the effect of seeing Alicia earlier that day, found myself remembering, in a long-ago summer, another evening.

Frank and I had played basketball in Whitaker Park until dark, removing then to the Calvetti home on Bell Street, not far from where I now sat. We sprawled, sixteen-year-old oafs, on the grass beneath a pear tree in the backyard. He was insisting on the superiority of the Yankees to the Dodgers. I only half listened, distracted by the girl sitting on the back steps, his suddenly deeply disturbing sister.

From the street came the cries of children playing, from next door the click-click of a lawn sprinkler. Music from radios oozed out of doors open against the warm night. Millers fluttered around rhomboids of light spilling from kitchen and parlor windows. A faint breeze stirred the leaves and the ripening fruit above us. The night was quietly, insistently alive.

The grass was cool. The stars sparkled. The girl on the steps was silent but not quite still.

The deepening shadows reduced life to an overwhelming moment and Alicia Calvetti's quiet breathing.

That was then: summer nights in small desert towns, swollen with promise.

This was now: I went to bed.

THREE

The next morning I awoke sluggish and, when I thought of my promises to Alicia Barnes and Mia Dunn, cranky. I was retired. I had my routines. I didn't do this sort of thing anymore.

In penance for my petulance, I strained my way through a workout at St. Mary's Fitness Center. Cleaned up and breakfasted, I called Frank but got no answer. Then I left, drove across town and into Sparks. A few jigs and jogs took me to the Pyramid Lake Highway.

Easing over a low desert ridge, the road slid into Spanish Springs Valley, until fairly recently a narrow stretch of playa edged with scrub and sage that crawled up the foothills of the Pah Rah Range. The playa was still there, an emptiness centering a choke of the same sort of strip malls and tract housing now gagging the South Meadows. Businesses were mostly chains and franchises. The new homes differed in details of façade or landscaping, which served only to emphasize their sameness. In the hazy distance, the mountains seemed smeared, unreal.

At the north end of the valley, the highway narrowed to climb over a juniper-spattered slump in the hills and then drop down to, eventually, the National Wild Horse and Burro Center, where, in a series of large corrals, animals stood unmoving, shaggy heads bowed as if in sleep or submission.

I turned off the highway, bypassed a knot of shabby homes stuck forlornly in the middle of nothing, and followed a dirt road that angled across the base of Warm Springs Mountain. The autumn had seen scattered rain showers but no snow so far, and now in drought the sparse sage seemed desiccated, the land dead.

I hadn't gone far down the dirt road when I began to smell, faintly, burn. After a mile or so, I came to a graveled drive up to a bench of land that jutted from the hillside. A small sign read "Stafford Cabinetry," but I could see only, as if painted there by Edward Hopper, a narrow, two-story, white, blue-shuttered house with a pillared porch and a single gable. As I pulled onto level ground, in the gable window a gray shadow shifted.

The lot was dominated by a large white metal building that also bore the sign for the cabinetry shop. Across from it, what was left of an old barn offered ash to the occasional gust of wind. In the middle of the char, a shovel-wielding man in rubber boots and gray coveralls and USMC cap stood watching me.

A new Audi and an old Ford pickup sat under a carport. I pulled up behind the truck, the rear window of which displayed a decal of an eagle, globe, and anchor. I climbed out, walked across the lot, and offered a shibboleth: "Semper Fi."

He was a few years my junior, midsized, wiry. His features were sharp, his hazel eyes clear. He looked me over, carefully, as if I might intend injury. "Nam? Who were you with?"

"Mike Three Five."

His nod didn't disturb the fine layer of sawdust on his cap. He cleared his throat. "Two Two. Snuck twenty in between Nam and Desert Storm."

"A Marine's a Marine, whenever," I said. "Especially those who don't make it."

We stood silent for a moment, the spontaneous somber ritual of the returned.

"What happened here, anyway?"

From the ruin wafted the smell of burned wood soured by acrid chemical fumes. Now in the rubble I could perceive cans, some exploded, of resins and oils and finishes, and blackened piles that still carried the configurations of stacked wood, some of this protruding from under scorched and partially collapsed walls and roof.

"The fire marshal says arson. Night before last."

"Lucky the embers didn't start something big." Even in the November chill, the desert was fire awaiting a spark.

"Whoever did this probably didn't much care what they started."

His tone suggested that the remark was preamble to explanation, but he offered nothing more.

"No question about it being arson?"

"Wasn't trying to hide it, the fire marshal says. Accelerant all over." He looked grim, like a man prepared to do battle. With a painful sounding rasp, he cleared his throat. "We were sleeping. Old furnace makes a racket, can't hear a damn thing."

I asked the obvious question. "Who would do this?"

He shrugged. He seemed tired.

I took out and handed him a card like that I'd given to Mia Dunn. "Jack Ross. I'm a retired P.I. I'm looking for the son of Howie Ragatz. That would be Newton Ragatz?"

"P.I." He considered my card. He considered me. "Attorney too. Staff officer, I suppose, in Nam. Regiment? Division?"

"Platoon commander," I said. "I was a grunt."

He hesitated. Something about me troubled him. But then he offered his hand. "Merle Stafford. Newt's my stepson. He's in the house."

Without asking me about my business with Newton Ragatz, he led me to the verandah. On one side of the front door hung a white wooden swing; on the other, white wicker chairs were arranged around a white wrought-iron table.

He slipped out of his rubber boots, coughed weakly. "Mind if we talk out here? Don't want to track up the house. I'll get Newt."

I sat quietly, waiting. A bit of breeze freshened the smell of fire.

The porch commanded a fine view of the desert in a thin, blue-gray haze: Warm Springs Valley, sage and alkali mud and a few old homes, which from this distance looked to be mere smudges on the land; then, beneath layers of colored rock formed of ancient siltings, the passage that led to Pyramid Lake; and, farther off, Palomino Valley, where on large brushy lots more homes, newer, were laid out in a relentless advance toward the mountains.

Merle Stafford stepped out of the door with a young man. Newton Ragatz too had on gray coveralls and a Marine Corps ball cap. He had my card in his hand. "Semper fi."

At first glance, he seemed an unlikely Marine—small, slim, soft-spoken. His facial features were delicately boned: he was nearly pretty, his small smile nearly sweet. But he had fought. Now everything about him spoke of caution. His quiet ease was actually alertness. The steady sweep of his pale blue eyes reconnoitered.

When he moved to the table to take a seat, he limped, slightly. He wore heavy laced boots, one built up.

We talked of the Corps. Merle Stafford, whom his stepson was pleased to call Gunny, had done twenty and run. The young man was a year back from Afghanistan, where he'd lost half of his left foot to an IED. He thought himself one of the lucky ones.

Eventually he said, "So what does a private detective want with me?"

"I haven't been a P.I. for years," I said. "I'm just doing a favor." Then quietly, tersely, mentioning only his father's name, I told him.

He listened carefully, as if to ensure that he didn't miss anything. When I finished, he said, "So there's a girl whose mother just died, the girl might be my dad's daughter, and you want to compare her DNA to mine, is that it?"

"To confirm paternity," I said. "Or not."

He nodded, as if to himself. "Sure, I don't mind. I mean, she might be my sister."

"There's your mother, Newt." With another rasping sound, Merle Stafford cleared his throat, then looked at me. "Laurel, my wife, I don't want to upset her."

I could see how the subject might be as painful for Laurel Stafford as it was for Alicia Barnes.

"I certainly won't do anything to distress her, Gunny. I can set up the appointment with the DNA lab. Your wife wouldn't have to meet or speak with the young woman. She wouldn't need to know about any of this unless you chose to tell her."

Merle Stafford was still troubled. "You might want to think about this, Newt."

The young man stood silently frowning, as if conducting an inner conversation. I again felt his caution.

"I guess I'd want to know who I am too. But I won't let any harm come to Mom, or to—what's her name, this nurse?"

"Mia. Let's just leave it at that for now, shall we?"

He didn't protest. He rose, as if about to leave. Then he said to his stepfather, "The crazy woman?"

Merle Stafford looked out over the desert. He coughed softly. "Sometime back, we got a couple of phone calls, late at night. She was drunk, foul, making accusations. Newt answered the first one. I got to the others so my wife didn't hear the filth."

Newt nodded again, again in a sort of self-confirmation. "She went on about my dad, said he loved her, not mom, they were running off together, he'd never have betrayed her. She—"

"Drunk talk," Stafford interposed. "Wild stuff. Drugs. Murder. Crazy."

"Mia's mother made drunken calls for a year or so before her accident," I said.

Newt's small smile was tinged with sadness. "Then I feel sorry for her. Mia, I mean."

He gave me his cell number. Then he stepped off the porch. "I have to stain a cabinet. Let me know where to go for the test."

He walked toward the metal shed. His limp was hardly noticeable. Something about his posture said that he was in want of a weapon.

The breeze had quickened. Ash stirred, dust scurried across the lot. Far out in the desert, a whirl of wind slowly dissipated. I wasn't eager to leave.

"Unusual house to find out here," I said.

Merle Stafford nodded. "Somebody built it a hundred years ago. Don't know what they were thinking. And it takes keeping up. But Laurel wanted a house. Not a trailer, not a cabin, a house. I had one."

"Lonely spot," I said.

"We like it." He paused to marshal both his words and his emotions. "She's happy here."

Then the door opened and, as if summoned, a beautiful woman appeared.

She was small and slender. Her hair was prematurely white. Her skin was nearly white too, and smooth, her eyes pale blue, her features like her son's, delicately boned. She was lightly made up, wore bits of jade at her ears and a jade choker at her throat and a light gray-green dress and a small linen apron and white heels. Her fragrance was faint, floral.

Laurel Stafford was fifty or so, but the white hair and skin made her seem strangely, artificially, ageless. In the shadows of her porch she was all earnest stylishness. Carrying a tray on which rested a pot of coffee, cups, cream and sugar, she might have stepped from an ad in a 1950s magazine for women.

I rose as her husband introduced us.

She placed the tray on the table. For a moment she inspected my extended hand as if it might contain or constitute a threat. Her own hand was soft and dry and exerted no pressure. Her smile was empty.

"Mr. Ross is here to see Newt," Stafford said.

When she looked at me blankly, I said: "Nothing important. An excuse to drive out into the desert, mostly. But I had to go a lot farther to find it than I used to."

She smiled her empty smile.

We sat. She poured coffee, served us. The action had about it a faux formality, like that of a little girl playing house.

"Thank you," I said.

"Yes," she said. She said no more. Her silence seemed not merely reserve.

"The barn," I began. "This place was a ranching operation?"

Her husband took it up. "There's good wells, and a spring over the slope. They ran a few cows. Somebody wanted to raise horses. Another guy tried chukar. My uncle thought he could make it with goats. Then for a long time the house was rented, but the place wasn't worked."

It was the property that brought Merle Stafford to Nevada, he said. His uncle died and left him the house and lot and surrounding acres. When he retired from the Corps, he'd come up from San Diego, thinking to sell, but realized the land was worth hanging onto. He discovered that he liked the area, quickly found a job working for a cabinetry outfit, and began to party.

"Those days are long past, of course." He lay his hand on his wife's forearm.

She sat silent and stiff. She was, I saw then, disengaged.

As if to confirm that assessment, she stood, offered me another empty smile, turned and went back into the house.

I tested the coffee, even as I gave Merle Stafford an enquiring look.

"She doesn't mean to be rude," he said evenly, after a brief cough. "She doesn't socialize a lot these days. She's a little uncertain with company."

I wasn't sure what he was telling me. He wasn't ready to say more.

Then we watched his stepson come out, cross to the pickup, and retrieve a tool.

"The foot bother him much?" Walking back, he seemed almost to patrol.

"Pains him some, sometimes," Stafford said.

"Any other problems?" I knew the statistics on vets of the Middle East wars: suicides, addictions, pathologies.

"Wanders off once in a while. Trouble sleeping. When he first got back, he had a couple, well, not fights, really, flashbacks I guess. Then he had some trouble in a bar—a drunk came up behind him, bumped him, Newt choked him out." He watched the young man enter the shop.

"Serious?"

"Could of been worse. He could of killed him. Guy sobered up and didn't press charges." A waft of breeze stirred the air, sounded almost like a sigh. "He doesn't go out much anymore. Not ready yet."

Newt disappeared into the shop.

"I was lucky," Stafford said. "Never had readjusting problems. Except once I'd processed out, I sort of forgot who I was for a while."

It was my turn to gaze out into the desert. "I didn't have any problems either, or so I thought—at least, I didn't connect my problems with Nam. I spent a lot of time in the desert. Had the occasional bad dream. And I was wound pretty tight. But I was running, hiding. Twenty years later, Nam caught up and kicked hell out of me."

"Newt has them once in a while, the dreams" he said.

I didn't want to think about all that. "Newt's dad, Howie Ragatz, did you know him?"

He took up his glass. "We partied. Howie was a champ at it. He had… resources."

I took a not very wild guess. "He was your coke connection?"

"And friend. I liked Howie, even if I didn't like the way he treated his wife. He didn't see she needed somebody to take care of her." He rose. "After he disappeared, even before, to be honest, I started to. Just a friend, at first. She made me remember I was a Marine."

"What do you think happened to him?"

"I don't know," he said. "Laurel thought drug dealers killed him. Could be. He always talked about getting into the business big time. She couldn't believe he'd just run off, but he might of. But lot of people were looking for him, not just cops. You know a guy named Maglie?"

"We've met," I said.

"And then there was an asshole named Kohler. Joe Kohler. He was giving Laurel a hard time, scaring her, threatening, until I ran him off."

"Don't know him." I said. "I assume you know about Gale Dunn?"

"Figured she must be who you were talking about—the girl's mother. The crazy woman."

"She was all alone, and alcoholic, out on a hardscrabble alfalfa farm, living with a brain malformation that could kill her at any moment." I wasn't sure where my sudden sympathy was coming from. "That'd be enough to drive a lot of us crazy."

He coughed his soft cough. At my look, he said, "Cold. Just getting over it."

He looked again out to the desert. "I knew about her. Laurel never. She knew Howie partied. She'd worked in clubs, seen the coke-whores, knew what went on. But the dancer, no. She doesn't know even yet." He stood and looked at me. "I'd like to keep it that way."

I saw again that he was tired, somehow reduced. And concerned. Caring for his wife took a lot out of him, it seemed.

I rose, took his offered hand. "I'm glad to have met you, Gunny."

We stepped down from the porch and walked to my car. The remains of the barn looked not so much burned as blighted.

As I opened the door, he spoke, "You figure he's dead? Howie?"

"I don't know," I said. "To be honest, I don't really care. Now that Newt has agreed to help, I don't need him."

"If he is dead," he said, not quite casually, "it'd be murder."

"Probably," I said

"You retired from private investigations, you said. Still a lawyer?"

"I never practiced law," I said, "but officially, yes, I'm a member of the bar."

"If anybody ever finds out Howie was murdered," he said, "maybe I'll need you."

I couldn't see where he was going with this.

"Cops would look for who got the most from his death, wouldn't they?"

I watched him. "Yes."

Then Gunnery Sergeant Merle Stafford, USMC, Ret., slowly shifted into attention. "That'd be me."

On the drive home, I found myself thinking about the three people I'd found on Warm Springs Mountain. I didn't know what to make of Laurel Stafford, the *Ladies Home Journal* costume and airs, the empty smiles and silences. And her son, wounded in body, perhaps in spirit, communing cautiously with himself. And Gunny Stafford, who I suspected knew more about the barn fire—about everything—than he let on.

Not that it mattered. Not to me. I was retired. I didn't do that sort of thing anymore.

Back at the house, I had lunch, then called Mia Dunn, who answered after a single ring. When I told her that I'd found Howie Ragatz's son, and that he'd agreed to provide DNA, she squeaked with pleasure. "Oh, that's wonderful. He'd be my brother? What's his name?"

"Let's not get ahead of ourselves," I said. "We won't know anything till we do the tests."

"Yes, you're right?" But she couldn't contain her excitement. "Who is he?"

I tried to explain. "There are other people, innocent people, involved in this, Mia. They know only your first name. You know only his last. I think we should leave it at that, at least until we know for sure that there's a connection."

"I see?" she said, disappointed. She had much riding on this. I hoped not too much.

I told her that I'd have technicians call her to set up an appointment.

As soon as she clicked off, I phoned a lab, explained what I wanted, arranged for them to contact both Mia Dunn and Newton Ragatz, asked that they let me know when they had results, and gave them a credit card number.

Finished, I realized that at least for now I had nothing to do. Maybe I had, on this matter, nothing more to do, period. Maybe I'd gotten lucky.

If Howie Ragatz had fathered Mia Dunn, she would be happy to have this confirmed. Newton Ragatz wouldn't be unhappy, and his mother need never know. Alicia Barnes would have her mind eased about her husband's fidelity and, perhaps, she might regard me with less distrust.

I thought about having a beer, but instead I simply sat in my chair, considering. I began to drift off. My phone rang, bringing me back.

Frank had something for me.

FOUR

A few minutes later I was across the river. When Frank didn't answer my knock, I walked around and found him on his patio, sitting with Paltry in the sun, drinking tea. As I took a seat, he rose and went inside, returning with a cup and saucer and a folder. He slid the folder across the table. "Howie Ragatz."

I looked quickly through the papers: copies of reports on Howie Ragatz's arrest for drug possession; standard bail-bond forms; a Missing Person report and follow-ups, notations, and comments; a Failure to Appear notice; and brief accounts of subsequent official investigations. A clump of newspaper clippings.

Frank kept me silent company, breathing in little gasps and gulps, as I drank tea and read the file. It filled in what he had outlined the day before.

As a White Pine High School pitcher, Howie Ragatz had developed a fast ball that earned him a scholarship to UNR, where he partied as hard as he threw, until, with a couple student members of a rowdy group who called themselves Sundowners, he was arrested for marijuana possession. As happened often with jocks, strings were pulled, the charge went away, and he found himself in the army. After serving an uneventful hitch, he returned to Reno and tried UNR again, but he dropped out after a year to work in the clubs. At the time of his disappearance, he had been dealing twenty-one at the Claim Jumper Casino. He was nearly thirty, three years married to a Harrah's cocktail waitress, the father of a two-year-old son.

Howie Ragatz had been stopped for speeding early one morning. A routine search of the car uncovered a packet of white powder wedged between the rear seat cushions. He was arrested and charged with cocaine possession. After his wife found a thousand dollars to buy a bail bond, a public defender managed to get the court date set back while Ragatz unsuccessfully sought the money to hire an expensive private attorney, one who would see that his sentence, rather than a term in prison, was probation and a counseling program.

When he failed to show for his court date, authorities looked for him, but not very hard.

They talked to his employers past and present. As a twenty-one dealer, Howie Ragatz was fast and sure and friendly but unreliable. He had been let go from Harrah's and Circus Circus for missing shifts, and Bryce Ragatz, owner and manager of the Claim Jumper, admitted that he had kept Howie on longer than he should have because he was a relative, although distant, and because he was a vet, and because he liked him—liked him so much, in fact, that he loaned his wife the thousand dollars for the bail bond.

In fact, everybody liked Howie Ragatz. He enjoyed a good time, and he never turned down a toot or a frolic with women attracted by his smile or his cocaine. A few of his friends allowed that he dealt not only cards but also coke, small time, enough to finance his own consumption. Some said he often spoke of wedging into the big-money drug trade. Others said that he sometimes expressed resentment that Bryce Ragatz had not invited him into family activities and standing. Most found his marriage a mystery. Several repeated the rumor that he had a girlfriend, an exotic dancer at the Blue Flame. No one at the topless club on Lake Street admitted to having ever heard of Howie Ragatz.

His wife had last seen him when he left their Sun Valley mobile home to go for cigarettes one evening. When he didn't come home, she was, she said, at first angry but not concerned—her husband liked a good time. When she learned that he had missed a shift, and then another, she grew fearful that he would once again lose his job. By the third day, when she finally called the sheriff, she was said to be in shock. She was convinced that Howie was dead, probably killed in some sort of drug deal. Their marriage was troubled, but surely he would never abandon her and their son, whom he doted on. He had to be dead.

Airport security found his car in the long-term parking lot. Nothing in the vehicle assisted the official investigation. There was no record of him having taken a flight out of Reno.

The law would go no further. The demands on limited resources were constant, and Howie Ragatz was, finally, of little matter when robbers and rapists and killers were about. The customary notifications went out, and the authorities turned their attention to other cases.

As Frank had said, the newspapers made much of all this. They couldn't run so much as a paragraph notice without labeling Howie the "nephew" of Carl and "cousin" of Bryce Ragatz, seeming to suggest that this gave him and his story special status.

"How'd you manage this?" I asked Frank. "I'm impressed."

"Luck." Frank's scowl couldn't mask his bright-eyed pleasure. "Turns out detectives working old cases had looked at him not long ago for armed robbery."

The only crime, other than murder, that in Nevada had no statute of limitations. "Who do they think he robbed?"

Frank nearly smiled then. "They think he might have robbed his cousin Bryce."

I remembered the Bryce Ragatz robbery. Three armed men in masks had surprised him and his driver in the alley behind the Claim Jumper. Somehow shooting started. The driver was hit and dropped his gun, and Bryce Ragatz picked up the pistol and shot and killed one of the robbers. The other two escaped with his attaché case, which contained, he said, only business papers. No one knew what the robbers thought they were getting.

According to Frank, RPD detectives had recently realized what those working the case twenty-five years before hadn't: the robbery of Bryce Ragatz and the disappearance of Howie Ragatz had occurred on the same day.

"Easy to see why it'd slip past them," Frank said. "The wife didn't report him missing for a couple of days. Then she went to the sheriff, who has jurisdiction in Sun Valley. RPD should have made the link, but they were focused on the dead guy, a local hard case named Dick Pym. They tied Pym to another thug, a Joe Kohler, but he alibied up. They never got a line on anybody else. Howie Ragatz was never mentioned."

Joe Kohler. I'd now heard the name twice in the same day.

"It's iffy, Frank," I said.

He didn't trouble himself to shrug. But he was interested, and it showed. I could think of only one way to keep him engaged.

"I don't suppose you could get the file?"

"Probably not," he said. "Missing person is one thing. Armed robbery is another. But I could talk to a few people."

"Why don't you."

I didn't care who had robbed Bryce Ragatz or what Howie Ragatz might have done, other than to have fathered Mia Dunn, but I wanted to keep Frank engaged, alert, bright-eyed.

Back home, I got on the computer. Joe Kohler wasn't hard to find. He lived in an older Sparks neighborhood. He'd done time for B & E and possession of stolen goods, had been questioned about, I noted, arson and extortion, and arrested more than once for assault, charges dropped. He'd slowed down recently, rheumatoid arthritis placing him in a wheelchair.

I knew where to go if I wanted to talk to him. At the moment, I didn't.

I thought about calling Alicia, but I'd learned nothing about Randy's activities, wouldn't have anything to tell her until the results of the DNA comparison came back. That wouldn't happen, the lab technician had told me, for a day or two. I got back to my life, such as it was.

I spent the rest of the afternoon on errands. I was watching the early evening news—war and terrorism abroad, corruption and political inanity at home—and thinking about what to cook for my dinner, when I heard a car pull into my driveway. The rap on my door came shortly.

He was big but carried his bulk lightly. I guessed mid-forties. With his dark hair slicked back, in black trousers and satin jacket, he looked like a seal, sleek. He drove a BMW like Alicia's, his black.

His smile would intimidate. "Len Maglie wants to see you."

My smile would negate the threat. "I don't much want to see him."

His smile widened. "Sure you do."

I considered him. He looked soft, but probably wasn't. He looked intelligent, and probably was.

I didn't want to mess with him. He was too big. I was too old.

"Hang on," I said.

He followed me into my office. As I unlocked the desk drawer, he said, "You'll want to be real careful what you pull out of there."

The teak box with the .38 in it lay beneath papers and files. But I didn't want the pistol. I wanted the photograph Mia Dunn had sent Alicia Barnes. Because that had to be, somehow, what this was about.

I showed it to him. He smiled his smile.

In the hallway, I grabbed my jacket. "I'll follow you."

He seemed about to object. He looked at me. Then he smiled. "Yeah, you probably will."

Evening shadows crawled up the Sierra as I drove south again, the black BMW towing me to North Virginia Street. "The Biggest Little City in the World" sign arched over absence. A couple of free-form sculptures occupied otherwise empty space. Traffic on the street was light, on the sidewalks, lighter. Downtown Reno was in decline, having lost the play of Northern Californians to reservation casinos on the other side of the mountains. A few of Reno's establishments still enticed tourists with special events, but others were boarded up or had been converted to hotels or condos. The Riverside now housed artists. The Mapes and the Nevada Club and Harold's Club were no longer there.

Over on Lake Street, the Blue Flame, I knew, was gone. Where topless dancers had humped poles and hustled drunks while Harvey Prior arranged crimes and dispensed dope, a consignment store now shopped used furniture. Prior was gone as well, first into Arizona retirement, then into the grave. Prostate cancer had killed him, but giving up his operations had saved him, word was, from his son-in-law, Len Maglie, tired of waiting and ready to take over.

Len Maglie had been Prior's main negotiator, persuader, and enforcer. Frustrated by his father-in-law's refusal to upgrade and expand his sex-selling activities, he took over and did it himself. Harvey Prior had been a crook who ran a few women. Len Maglie was a pimp who had a few other business interests. He'd been and no doubt still was a very dangerous man.

I followed the black BMW to a narrow street off Gentry Way and a mostly empty parking lot beside two stories of brick formerly occupied by a discount electronics store. Above the entrance, the name of the club flickered in neon: Off Limits.

While I parked, my escort waited at the door, beside which brass plates announced that the club provided adult entertainment and admitted members only. We stepped inside.

I let my vision adjust to the dimness. A foyer opened onto a large room all dark wood and plush fabrics: a square bar, tables and booths arranged around a stage outfitted with chromed poles, several elevated platforms from which couches and stuffed chairs looked onto smaller stages. The walls were papered in shades of red and hung with long mirrors. The air was cool, smelled antiseptic.

"All the comforts of home," I said.

"Makes a buck." The big man gave the room an almost proprietorial survey. "Could do a lot more."

At the moment, the club wasn't doing much of anything. A bartender in a white shirt and formal black-tie polished glasses. A young woman wearing an evening gown that revealed the colorful tattoos on her shoulders and lower back selected CDs from a rack beside a huge sound system. Another young woman in halter and hot pants wiped at a booth table. Before a closed door stood a block of a man, square of head and jaw and shoulders, from the left sleeve of whose tuxedo poked not a hand but a thick pad of black hard rubber that would do serious damage.

Then the closed door opened as a voice rumbled into the room. "Ross, you fuck. I thought you were dead."

Len Maglie was my age, six inches shorter but wider, with broad shoulders and wedge-like back. His gray suit was beautifully cut, smoothed over hard muscle.

"Just retired," I said.

"Miracle you lived long enough to retire," he said, moving into the room.

Len Maglie was an ill-favored man, his head bald and bumpy, his features lumped and not quite aligned, but his grin rearranged his face and gave him an ugly charm. His voice sounded as if he spoke from the bottom of a deep well.

"First time I ever see this fuck, Snooks, he says he'll kill me."

The big man smiled. "Didn't manage it, looks like."

"Memory goes when you're getting old, they tell me," I said. "Maybe that's why I don't quite recall it that way."

One of my first jobs after I finished active duty and law school and returned to Reno had me looking for the daughter of a Sacramento mortician. I found her at the Blue Flame, dancing, snorting coke, turning tricks. She was fifteen. I made a deal with Harvey Prior: the young woman would come with me and I wouldn't tell anyone where I found her. Len Maglie then promised that, should the authorities hear about her activities at the club, I would suffer. I'd rejoined that if he came after me, he'd better kill me. Otherwise, it was the last thing he'd ever do.

"Threatens me in front of my father-in-law. Crazy fuck." Maglie grinned. "You were really crazy, weren't you?"

"I sure was, by golly."

Len Maglie's grin spread. "Still crazy, Ross?"

"I'm much better, thanks," I said. "As far as getting better goes, you've upped your game considerably. Compared to that sticky, smelly, slimy sex pit you used to run, this operation looks almost civilized."

"Times change. Business changes or dies."

"Like some people," Snooks said, smiling at me again.

"If you're retired," Maglie said, "how come you're pestering my people?"

I didn't know what he meant, exactly, but it didn't matter. I took out the photograph of the four people in the round booth. "Favor for a friend."

Maglie took it, looked at it. "Fuck," he said. "Come on back."

We stepped into a hallway, at each end of which rose a narrow staircase to the second floor. Three doors interrupted one wall. The first two were closed. The third door opened to Len Maglie's office. It was small and tidy, contained the usual machines, as well as a wall of closed-circuit television monitors offering views of several rooms, which I assumed were upstairs, furnished for comfort and, no doubt, cavorting. Three of the screens showed the big room we'd just left.

"Okay," he said, sitting. "How come you're asking about Gale Dunn and Howie Ragatz?"

I didn't bother to point out that I hadn't asked him about anyone. "I'm inquiring about all of them," I said. "What can you tell me?"

"Why should I tell you anything?"

"For old times' sake?" When he didn't smile or answer, I added, "You might not have heard. She's dead. Got drunk and fell off a tractor."

He placed the photograph on the desk. "Yeah. Gale. Howie Ragatz had a hard-on for her. His cousin too. So did the money magician there—what the fuck's his name? Burns?"

"What was so special about her?"

"Nothing," he sneered. "Oh, she had a way about her. Arrogant bitch. Thought because Harvey took her out and about once in a while she shouldn't have to work the clientele like the other bimbos, squirm around on laps like Tab there. You wouldn't want to be under old Tabby's squirm these days."

The man he'd called Snooks came in and took up a position just at the edge of my vision.

Maglie frowned. "So how come you got a little girl doing your work for you?"

I began to understand. Mia Dunn. Tabby Sabich. Len Maglie.

I shrugged. "I work alone, Len. You know that."

"What I fucking know, Ross, is that Gale Dunn is dead," he said, "and Tabby is old and fat, and the money man—"

"Barnes," I said. I took up the photo, looked at my dead friend's dazed, dazzled grin. "His name was Randal Barnes. He's dead too."

"And the only one left is Howie Ragatz." Maglie leaned back in his chair. "He the one you're looking for, is he?"

"No, not really," I said, placing the photograph back on the desk. "Word is he's probably dead. I don't know otherwise."

"Course you'd say if you knew," Maglie said, grinning now.

I grinned back at him. "Howie Ragatz dealt a little coke. Back then, you and Harvey were known to dabble in the business, as I recall."

The room got very quiet. Snooks took a deep breath. Then Maglie slowly grinned.

"You still push, don't you, Ross?" When I shrugged, he went on. "Nobody ever proved we had anything to do with drugs."

"It wasn't much of a secret," I said, pushing a tad more, riding a familiar rush: adrenaline. "But that was a long time ago, and I'm just a retired old P.I. doing a favor for a friend."

He raised his big, high-knuckled, liver-spotted right hand, slowly folded his fingers, and turned his fist one way, then the other, as if admiring a prized possession. "What kind of favor? For who?"

I smiled. "That would be a private matter."

"Not very private," he said. "It's the kid, ain't it, Gale's kid?"

I didn't say anything.

"Or Howie's wife," he said. "Like one of them china dolls, she used to be. Look at her wrong, she'd crack apart."

I didn't respond.

Len dropped his hand. "Doing favors. I could do you one, maybe. But you'd have to do me a favor too."

I shrugged. "If I can."

"Howie Ragatz." His grin went hard. "I want to know if he's dead or alive, and if he's alive I want to know where he is. And if he's got any money left, I want it back."

"What money is that?"

Now his grin vanished and he became ugly, ugly and mean. "My money."

"I'm not looking for Howie Ragatz."

"You are now, Ross." He sat back, turned to the big man. "Have Paulie come in."

I was being dismissed. Snooks, smiling, gestured for me to step past him. I didn't much like giving him my back, but when I did, nothing happened.

He walked me down the hall to the main room. Now four men in sport coats were settled in a booth watching a topless, bikini-bottomed, elaborately tattooed young woman in rhythm to a Bruno Mars serenade twine herself around a pole.

The square man looked on impassively. Snooks spoke to him. "He wants you."

We crossed the room. I opened the door to near darkness. To my surprise, Snooks followed me out. "Maglie. You knew him from before. How good was he?"

At mayhem, he meant. "I never saw him in action. Word was, he was as good as they come."

"I heard that too." Something pulsed in his eyes.

"You wouldn't be thinking of finding out for sure?"

He smiled. "I'm as loyal as the day is long."

I remembered his remark as we had entered. "You think business might be better with a change of management?"

His smiled changed. "Now, I didn't say that. You didn't hear me say that, did you?"

"No," I said. "I guess not."

"Right." He took my arm, directed me toward my car. "Best idea he ever had, getting out of the dope business. It's a mess these days—all the pills, home-brew meth, all that. This place, on the other hand, is a cash cow. But the cash doesn't get put to work."

"You sound like an MBA."

He grinned. "He's a good boss, Maglie. Even if he's like old Harvey Prior was. Satisfied."

I knew what he meant. Harvey Prior enjoyed being out, around town, in Vegas, in the Bay Area, at fights and shows and events, with women on his arm and maître d's at his elbow, spending money, being seen and served. His sex and dope operations paid for his pleasures, and he had never shown any inclination to expand. If Maglie now felt the same, an ambitious employee might be watching, carefully, for the opportunity to advance his own interests.

"As loyal as the day is long," I repeated with a smile.

I didn't point out to him that the day held only a few more hours.

Tired, a bit jittery from the adrenaline jolt, I decided to treat myself. In an Indian restaurant on South Virginia, I had a curry and a bottle of beer. Then I drove home again, got myself another beer, and took it to my chair.

I assumed that Mia Dunn had been in touch with Tabby Sabich. The young nurse must have used my name in the process. Ms. Sabich had reported to Len Maglie.

I only wanted to determine if Randal Barnes had been unfaithful to his wife. But now I was dealing with sleaze-merchants and thugs, concerning myself with long-gone men and missing money. I was doing things I didn't do anymore.

I felt an old, familiar urge. But I couldn't head for the desert. I'd made promises.

FIVE

The next morning, walking back from my run, sweated out but stuffed with endorphins, I resolved to not fret about Len Maglie and his muscle, about Mia Dunn, about Randy Barnes and Gale Dunn and Howie Ragatz. I would await the results of the DNA comparison, spend the next day or two in my retirement rut, puttering.

I was dusting in my living room, listening to Tony Bennett and k. d. lang, when my phone rang.

"Can we meet for lunch, Jack? One-ish, at Emile's?" Alicia sounded tense, agitated. "I know this is short notice, but it's important."

I could believe that it was important, at least to her. She hadn't phoned me in years, not since Cynthia was young. I assumed that this must have something to do with Randy, although I couldn't guess why we had to discuss matters over food.

"Yes," I said, "All right."

"Emile's? Do you know it?" As if my being familiar with a restaurant she frequented was highly unlikely, me being me.

"I'll find it," I said.

"Could you—it's not the sort of place diners wear jeans in."

Old habits. She must chide and correct, I must itch and chafe.

"I'll get my glad rags on," I said.

If she detected my irritation, she didn't say so. Instead, she offered, with apparent sincerity, gratitude. "Thank you, Jack. This is . . . well, thank you."

I spent more of the morning on chores. Then I cleaned up and made myself presentable in gray and cream and a tan corduroy jacket. Prepared as best I could for Alicia's world, I left.

Emile's, Google had told me, was even farther south than I'd been two days earlier. I gave myself plenty of time, but once off the freeway I had to take it slow. I didn't get lost this time, but I was still late.

The bistro was a recent enthusiasm of the local gentry, whose expensive automobiles gleamed in the parking lot. Around them, amid a few handsome trees the developer had spared, Spanish-style buildings bore discrete signs identifying upscale clothing emporia, law and realty offices, a plastic-surgery clinic, a wine boutique, and Emile's. Empty space between the units insisted, unpersuasively, that this was not just a fancy strip mall.

The soft light in Emile's dining room cast no shadows, the pale poppies on the wallpaper evoked Provence, and the air was sweetly scented, perhaps by the effluences of those—most but not all women—seated at the damask-draped tables. The ambience suggested surety, the security of entitlement.

A svelte, silk-clad hostess escorted me to Alicia's table.

I shaped an apologetic smile. "Sorry. Traffic."

Alicia looked great in a blouse of autumnal colors. She hadn't touched her Mediterranean salad. She curled her fingers tightly around the stem of a glass of white wine.

"No matter." She assessed my attire, might have approved. "Thank you for coming."

I turned to include in my smiling regrets the other woman at the table.

She was Alicia's age, I knew, even if she looked, at least at first glance, twenty years younger. But her hair was improbably dark and glossy, her face suspiciously smooth. Her saffron-colored sheath stretched from bony shoulders over an unlikely bosom. A clutch purse lay within reach.

"Carlotta, this is Jack Ross," Alicia said. "Jack—Carlotta Farragut Ragatz." Her tone proposed that I might want to genuflect, or at least bow.

Carlotta Farragut Ragatz didn't invite me to join them. She would have me stand in attendance to her. When she spoke, the muscles around her mouth barely quivered.

"After dealing with your simpering little emissary, I thought it best to confront you face to face, immediately."

Simpering little emissary. Mia Dunn, I thought.

"We won't be dragged into your gutter."

Her rudeness was deliberate, meant not to provoke but to underscore her disdain. She seemed to believe that she could give insult with impunity. Maybe she could. Alicia may have been nearly a pillar of society, but Carlotta Farragut Ragatz was a mover and a shaker.

For Alicia's sake, I accepted the abuse, managed to preserve my smile. "We've met, Mrs. Ragatz, although you probably don't remember. A teenage party at Pyramid Lake."

Several carloads of us had driven out to the desert lake to drink beer and feed a bonfire and frolic in the August night. Carlotta Farragut, about to fly off to a snooty Swiss school, had swigged beer, chased evanescent sparks around the fire, then got sick, then passed out.

"No," she said coldly. "I don't think so."

I shrugged and, uninvited, sat.

"You were some kind of athlete in high school." Her smile was stiff, might have actually been a sneer. "There was something else about you too, about your parentage. Your mother was a . . . what? Showgirl, that sort? She was killed in a drunken barroom fracas?" Her smile went even harder. "And you achieved your own nasty notoriety—for years we regularly read newspaper reports of your thuggish doings."

I smiled at Alicia, who seemed stunned by the unpleasantness. "Puked her guts out at that party, Lottie here. Hind end up in the air, front smeared with vomit, face pressed into the wet sand—made quite a picture."

Alicia, paling, swallowed wine.

Carlotta Farragut Ragatz did not deign to scowl. With her fork she picked at the wedge of quiche on her plate, seeming to find it as unsatisfactory as she found me.

Even in high school, she'd had an imperious air. She was not really pretty or particularly intelligent, but she was the daughter of Denny Farragut, a colorful gaming figure who'd made and lost several fortunes. Unlike Carl Ragatz, a businessman trained in accounting, Farragut was a gambler who trusted his instincts and his luck. Momentarily flush, he had, after allowing his daughter to attend Reno High for a year, shipped her off to Europe to what was then called a finishing school. Finished, she did a year at Smith before, returned for summer vacation, she managed to get pregnant by Bryce Ragatz. Their marriage proceeded even after the pregnancy was deemed false. The union was hailed as the merging of two legendary Northern Nevada gaming families. There ensued no more pregnancies, false or otherwise, but the marriage endured.

A waitress appeared at my elbow. "The quiche Lorraine is especially good today, sir."

I was hungry, but I wasn't ready to spend fifty dollars for a sliver of cheese and bacon bits. I asked for a cup of coffee.

Hiding behind her wine glass, Alicia seemed not to breathe as she watched me. I determined to behave, called up a quiet, balanced, businesslike tone.

"About my so-called emissary, Mrs. Ragatz. I assume you're referring to a young nurse named Mia Dunn."

"She thought she could barge into our home, babbling about my husband's cousin and you." She took up her own glass of wine. "I've dealt with the likes of her before. I've also dealt with your ilk."

"My ilk?" I could feel the heat rising up my neck.

She turned to Alicia, frowning formidably. "Would you give us a minute?"

Alicia put down her glass. "Yes, of course, I'll just go—"

I prepared to protest, but Alicia quickly rose and moved off across the room.

"Whom are you working for?" Carlotta Ragatz said brusquely. "What do you want?"

What I wanted was to get up and walk out. But I sat, regained my balance, and said, "I'm not working for anyone."

She didn't believe me. "I can have your license with one phone call."

"Maybe you could, if I had a license," I said. "I don't. What I do have is a request for help from a young woman who is trying to identify her father."

A flush stained her too-smooth cheeks. "And you want to pin it on my husband!"

"I don't want to pin anything on anyone." Before she could object, I told her about Mia's exotic-dancer mother, about the Blue Flame, about the money for support and education. As I spoke, I watched her slowly engage. I mentioned only one name.

"Howie Ragatz?" Arched brows expressed her interest. "A short while back, we—I got a phone call, a mad woman, drunk, vile. She talked about him, said . . ." She frowned, deciding not to tell me what the woman had said. Instead, she asked, "Howie was this girl's father?"

"He's a candidate," I acknowledged. "There are others."

"Including my husband?"

"Not really," I said, even as I recalled Len Maglie's list of men interested in Gale Dunn. "But I'd like to talk with him. He knows several of the people involved in this."

"My husband doesn't consort with prostitutes," she said haughtily.

That called for no response I cared to give.

The waitress brought my coffee.

Carlotta Farragut Ragatz issued her verdict: "If what you say is true, and the story is so unlikely it might very well be, then . . . but you can see why I thought . . ."

She glared, making her error my fault. "We've been approached by private detectives before. They imagined that we would pay to keep our private lives private. A serious blunder on their part."

"You thought I wanted to shake you down?"

She reassessed me, grudgingly. "Can you blame me? After all the stories?"

I ignored that, mostly because she had a point. "All I'll need is a few minutes of your husband's time."

She took a slow sip of wine: "You're fortunate. He's off flying, but he returns tonight. If he follows his usual habit, he'll be at the Stead airfield tomorrow morning, I'm sure, babying his plane. You can talk to him there."

"I will," I said. "Thank you."

Cutlery clanked softly against china. Alicia was nowhere to be seen.

"He . . . Howie Ragatz was a charmer, with that little smile of his." She pursed her lips as if preparing to expectorate. "It didn't work on me. I saw him for what he was, one more casino worker living at the edge of the criminal world—dope, sex, thugs and hijackers and robbers, the world you skulked about in."

She reached for her purse, pulled it toward her as if it offered protection. Then, abruptly, she said, "That phone call from the mad woman. Do you know anything about it?"

"The ex-dancer, the mother of the young woman I'm trying to help, she made calls like that. She died a couple of months ago."

She went silent for a moment. Then she said, "I don't doubt that Howie would father a child on some slut, especially with a wife like his. I encountered her once, when she was after Bryce for money for her husband's bail. Strange woman. Vapid."

I tried my coffee. It had grown lukewarm.

Carlotta Farragut Ragatz took from her purse a checkbook and a pen, wrote rapidly. I looked at the amount she'd filled in and laughed.

She ignored my reaction. "I want to know the results of your investigation. If it exposes evidence that might implicate my husband in this business, or in anything else for that matter, I want it kept confidential."

I held the check out to her. "I'm not conducting an investigation, Mrs. Ragatz. And as I said, I no longer have a valid P.I. license. I'm not for hire."

Again she seemed about to spit. "Everyone's for hire, Mr. Ross."

I didn't say anything.

"You want more, is that it?" She offered her sneering smile.

"I don't want anything." I held up the check, tore it in half, and in half again, and let the pieces flutter onto the expensive tablecloth. Theater, but it had its effect.

"I see," she said.

I gave her what I could. "I'm an attorney, Mrs. Ragatz, an officer of the court. If I come across evidence of illegal activities, I'm duty-bound to pass it on to the authorities. But other than that, I won't blab. I'll listen to gossip, but I won't pass it on. I wish neither you nor your husband ill."

That wasn't quite enough for her. "Are you a man of your word, Mr. Ross?"

Good question. I answered honestly. "I try."

That wasn't quite enough for her either, but she saw that it was all she was going to get. She gave me a card. "You can get me at this number at any time."

She rose. I rose too and watched Carlotta Farragut Ragatz swank out of the room.

Alicia almost magically materialized. "Jack, I didn't know, I never imagined she'd be so horrid," she said, sitting. "That about your mother was just meanness. I'm sorry."

"Merely a superficial wound," I said. Another joke she didn't get. I seemed unable simply to accept her sympathy.

She took up her fork. "I hope you don't think I got you here under false pretenses."

"No pretense," I said. "You asked me here, and here I am."

"Yes, here we are." Alicia looked slowly around the room, at the tables occupied by the stylish and cosseted and entitled, as if to assure herself that she was in the right place.

"Carlotta called and said she wanted to meet you. Well, who was I to deny her—she's Carlotta Farragut Ragatz, isn't she?" Alicia took a deep breath. "I'm chair of the Truckee Meadows Arts Council scholarship committee this year, Jack. And a word from Carlotta will open a lot of purses and wallets."

"Will you get that word?"

"With Carlotta you never know." She frowned again. "You finally got along?"

"We came to an understanding," I said.

"Oh," she said. She added, uncertainly, "Good."

She involved herself with her salad, I with my cold coffee. I searched for something to say.

"You were wrong about the jeans." I nodded at a man in designer denim across the room. "Mine don't run me five hundred dollars a pair, though."

She gave me a narrow look, as if suspecting a jibe. I smiled assurance to the contrary.

We sat in mutual unease. To relieve it, I told her what I'd been doing, whom I'd spoken with, what I'd learned. I told her about Mia Dunn and Newton Ragatz and the lab tests.

As the young nurse had, Alicia leapt ahead. "That means we won't need Randy's DNA after all?"

I shrugged. "Depends on how the lab comparison goes."

"But you think this Howie Ragatz is the girl's father?"

"If I had to bet, I'd put my money on him," I said. "But he isn't a sure thing."

Alicia and I lapsed into a silence of the unsaid. She moved bits of olive and pepper about on her plate. Then she put down her fork.

"Thank you for coming, Jack," she said almost formally. "And for making an effort with your clothes."

A quip came to mind, but I left it there. "You're welcome."

Her mouth softened. "You look nice, by the way."

"So do you, Alicia." It seemed to me that she had just shifted our relation. I took a chance. "You look good."

"The Italian diet, olive oil and garlic," she said. "Randy always joked that it would keep me young and him alive."

The thought of her dead husband and my dead friend silenced us both. Then came the question I'd been waiting for.

"Did he cheat on me with that woman? That dancer?"

I chose words carefully. "I haven't met anyone yet who says so."

Alicia looked around the room again, taking in the well-dressed, carefully kept, supremely satisfied diners, as if to reassure herself.

"Randy handled some tax things for Bryce Ragatz. He saved him a lot of money. That gave us an in with Carlotta. Randy didn't care for her, but he understood how important she could be. Brunch with Carlotta Farragut Ragatz would have seemed a … I don't know, certification, almost. But the invitation never came. For years I found it convenient to blame—what did Carlotta call it?—your 'nasty notoriety.' People read about you, your awful cases, and they knew we'd been married, they made me feel . . . tainted."

I had no response for that.

"Since Randy died, I've been odd woman out," she said quietly. "I'm often not included. I'm not always in the right place with the right people anymore."

I wasn't totally sure what she was telling me.

"But now the word will get out that I was here with Carlotta Farragut Ragatz."

"And you'll get back in to the right places," I said. "Be with the right people again."

I had meant to be encouraging. Alicia took it otherwise. Perhaps she heard something in my voice, saw something in my expression. Perhaps

I had, years earlier, said something similar but contemptuous. Or perhaps she had recognized her own condescension.

Her smile went hard. "You always disapproved of everything I wanted."

That was true, even if I wasn't going to say so. "We were just different people, Alicia. We had no common interests, no shared enthusiasms."

"Except in bed." Her defiant look dared me to deny it. "The only place I didn't bore you. And then you got bored even there, so you ran off to kill little Asian men."

I had nothing to say to that either

She smiled, bitterly. "But our daughter turned out well and happy, and I survived nicely, thank you. I made a good life with Randy."

"Yes." I was again struck by how well she had aged. Time left only light traces on her face, throat, hands. "You belong here."

She put down her fork. "Is that one of your clever jabs, Jack?"

"Alicia . . ."

I looked at her, saw the girl in the woman, a past life in the present.

Then I said what I'd wanted to say to her for years. "I'm sorry."

Her gaze narrowed.

I should have kept quiet. But I couldn't.

"I'm sorry for everything," I said. "For the pain I caused, the problems I created for you. I lied to you. I betrayed your trust. And I'm sorry."

She started to speak, then stopped. She wanted to say something, I sensed, but finally anger was easier. "Who are you trying to make feel better, Jack—me or yourself?"

It was a fair question. I couldn't answer it.

"Do you want me to forgive you, is that what you want? After all these years?"

"I don't *want* anything," I said louder than I intended. "It wasn't a request. It was a statement. I treated you badly. I did things, some worse than others, but—"

She was very angry. "The worst thing you did, Jack, was marry me."

To that I had no response that wouldn't cause pain.

We left.

Alicia didn't wait while I paid the outrageous bill. By the time I stepped out into the warming afternoon, her BMW was gone. For a while I sat in my car, trying to calm down.

Around Alicia, I seemed compelled to folly. Guilt, of course.

Carlotta Farragut Ragatz had questioned my trustworthiness. Alicia could only remind me of my great infidelity. And of what followed—my nasty notoriety.

I'd come back from Vietnam clamped in a kind of controlled hysteria.

I spent a lot of time in the desert, alone. In the desert, I could see for miles, so nothing could sneak up on or surprise me. There were no booby traps in the desert, no minefields, no sappers or snipers, only scorpions in their dark places and snakes that whirred warnings.

When I wasn't in the desert, when I was with other people, working, I did bad things to myself. I looked for and often found the ghastly, from which I took a tormented comfort. I killed, I shot two men and another I kicked to death. Some of this ended up in the newspapers. Several times I was interrogated by officers of the law.

My personal life wasn't much better. I feuded, mindlessly it now seemed, with my ex-wife. I acted out with women my distrust of all that I'd once hoped for. I loved my daughter, but I sometimes scared her. I tested, occasionally to anger, my only real friend. I adopted poses—taciturn westerner, Nevada good old boy, Stanford liberal, smart-ass P.I., and solitary desert rat—but I had no idea who or what I really was.

I still didn't, for certain. At the moment, I just felt small and stupid.

SIX

I drove home and made a lunch of Ritz crackers and cheddar cheese and apple slices, which I ate as I watched the noontime local news and weather.

A wet storm would arrive in a few days. Till then, it would be warmer than normal.

Temperatures at Reno/Tahoe International Airport were five degrees higher than forty years ago when it was surrounded by cool alfalfa fields, not tarmac and concrete.

Nevada was the fastest-growing state in the nation. The population of Washoe County was swelling. Temperatures would continue to rise.

I finished my lunch, debating what to do. I was floating in the backwash of my ineptness with Alicia and in no mood to talk to anyone, but Mia Dunn was out there trying to deal with unpleasant people. If she kept at it, she could get hurt.

I called her number. No answer. I called the hospital. She had taken a couple of personal days. I called Newt Ragatz. He too didn't answer. I called Merle Stafford, who did. He told me a story.

Early that morning, Merle and Newt were in the shop when they heard a car pull into the lot. Newt went out. After a while, Gunny Stafford heard an engine start up. He went to the door in time to see a small blue car leave the lot. The driver had frizzy red hair. Her passenger was Newton Ragatz.

"Mia Dunn," I told him.

He cleared his throat. "I thought this was all supposed to be anonymous."

"I thought so too."

I told him I'd find Newt and send him home.

My computer gave me, after a brief search, a number in Gardnerville for Gale Dunn. No answer there either.

I Googled directions to Mia's address. Fifteen minutes later I pulled into a parking space before her South Meadows apartment. Like much else in the area, the complex was relatively new and already shabby: buckled ersatz adobe shingles, begrimed spray-on plaster, rusting wrought-iron rails, and a few sad-looking yuccas.

Mia's car wasn't in the parking lot. She didn't answer my knock. The complex had no security system, and the lock on her door was uncomplicated. I was surprised at the relative ease of conscience with which I broke the law.

The apartment was obsessively tidy. The inexpensive furnishings showed no sign of wear, and the appliances might never have been used. Wall decorations—posters, photos—expressed only a desire to break up bareness. A shelf held nursing books, the coffee table a fan of magazines of the sort found in doctors' offices. The only personal item on display was the photograph, standing on a bedside table, of Gale Dunn sitting unsmiling on a tractor.

I wondered what it would be like to come home, day after day, to this. Mia Dunn's life seemed as boring as mine. I left.

Traffic on I-580 South thinned as I headed out of town. The new elevated concrete highway annulled nature, smoothed lumps and dips and straightened bends into detached, idealized forms. Even the Sierra seemed artificial, mere backdrop. Miles meaninglessly sped by until 580 passed Carson City and reverted to old 395 and took on the character of the land.

Desert and dust, scrubland scarred by dry washes, everywhere sage and rabbit brush, here and there piñon and juniper, old tracks and trails leading to hillside diggings, and the Sierra darkly, dramatically thrust up. I hadn't been down this way for a long time, had forgotten how empty and useless and pretty the countryside was.

Eventually the landscape changed, until the highway crept up a rise to expose a broad desert expanse patched with hayfields and pastures. Dirt roads angled off toward farm and ranch buildings. Billboards and signs cluttered. Ahead in the haze I could see the darkness of the trees and rooftops of Gardnerville and Minden.

While still some distance from town, I found the road that I wanted, and, down it a way, the Dunn place. The fields were well tended, and bright machines and clean shiny equipment lined up in an open shed. In contrast, the old house was in poor shape, roof sloppily patched, porch slanted, siding warped in places, screen door off center and not quite closed. A small blue car sat in the weak late-afternoon sunlight.

As I got out, the screen door opened. Mia Dunn appeared in the doorway, all eager innocence. "Do they know?"

The DNA lab, she meant. "Not yet," I said. "I haven't heard from them."

"I did," she said, "I mean I called? One of the technicians, I know her, she said it would probably be tomorrow, but I thought maybe . . . ?"

"No," I said. "This lab technician, she'd be the person who gave you Newt Ragatz's name and address?"

She nervously patted her frizz of hair but said nothing.

"I assume Newt's with you."

"He's inside." Wide-shouldered, deep-chested, her body effectively blocked the door.

"What have you been doing?" I asked quietly.

"Nothing," she said, flushing as if accused. "We didn't—we just talked."

"I don't mean that," I said. "I mean going to see Tabby Sabich and Carlotta Ragatz."

Again she patted her hair. "I just wanted to find out . . . but Tabby Sabich got angry, like I was getting her in trouble? And Mrs. Ragatz wouldn't even let me in."

"And with both of them, you used my name."

She couldn't meet my eye. "Yes, but, well, you did say you'd help, didn't you? So today we came here, to look, I thought . . . and we found another photograph?"

I waited, but she didn't go on. I suddenly felt weary. I didn't understand why I'd broken into her apartment. I had a bad feeling about all that I was doing. Doing what I didn't do anymore.

"I'd like to talk to Newt, Mia. May I come in?"

After a moment, she stepped aside.

The house was dim and chilly. The shabbiness of the exterior was repeated inside: stained walls, cracked linoleum, sagged and wobbly furniture. It smelled of old dust, rot. I thought of Gale Dunn, alone, like her house going to ruin.

In the kitchen, at a plastic-topped table, sat Newt Ragatz. He nodded, watchfully. Before him lay a photograph: Howie Ragatz, lolling in a hot tub, smiling his self-satisfied smile.

"It was under the lamp on her bedside table?" Mia assumed a protective posture beside the young man: he might have been her patient. "Where she could look at it at bedtime?"

There was nothing in the photo to suggest where it had been taken, or when.

Mia hovered. "She wouldn't have kept it there, would she, if she wasn't in love with him? And wouldn't that mean that he probably was my father?"

Her voice, still soft, thickened with emotion. She wanted this bond. As if to establish it, she placed a hand on Newt Ragatz's shoulder.

"I don't know," I said. "I do know that you've got to stop what you've been doing. Your mother knew some unfriendly people. You've stirred them up."

Newt listened carefully to our exchange. He seemed to take in each remark, assess it, and arrange it in relation to the others, as if at a briefing before a mission into the bush.

Now he spoke, quietly, as he rose from the chair. "These unfriendly people. My dad knew them? They're some kind of criminals?"

"The bad kind," I said. "The kind that hurt people."

Mia told me, at my inquiry, about her meeting with Tabby Sabich. Her mother's friend initially was pleased to see her, but she soon changed, her replies to Mia's inquiries becoming curt. She didn't want to talk about Howie Ragatz. Her boss, Len Maglie, wouldn't want her to. She warned Mia not to get involved in Howie Ragatz's disappearance.

"We were going to talk to Bryce Ragatz, maybe," Mia said. "He's not . . . I mean, I didn't know he was so important, his family and all?"

"Wait for the DNA," I said. Her ingenuous insistence was wearing on me. "Then, if it's not a match, I'll see him myself."

"But what can I—we, what can we do?"

I could understand her frustration. "I know it's difficult, Mia. Waiting."

"Yes. Difficult." Her eyes misted over. She placed her hand on Newt Ragatz's arm, as if for support.

"He's right," Newt said to her, quietly. He paused, as if in silent communion with himself. Then he turned to me. "Maybe you can give me a ride to Warm Springs?"

"Oh," Mia said, alarmed. "I can take you back."

"Not to Warm Springs." He gave her the photograph. "It's better that you don't go out there. Not until we know for sure. My mother . . ."

The young woman looked at him in dismay. "But I thought . . ."

"When we hear about the DNA, I'll call you," he said softly. He seemed now, like his mother, removed.

Mia looked at him, trying to believe him. Whether or not she succeeded I couldn't tell.

She stayed at Newt's elbow as he limped out to my car. She gave us a wan little wave goodbye, stood alone in the slanting sunlight as we pulled away.

On the drive back, Newt spoke quietly as he responded to my equally quiet prompts. He selected words with care, as if determined to get things right.

He liked Mia Dunn, and he felt sorry that her mother had made the girl unhappy, and he appreciated her eagerness to establish that his father was also hers. If he was. But if he was, Newt offered, she was getting no prize.

For himself, Newt had hoped to satisfy his curiosity: was Howie Ragatz as big a jerk as he seemed in the stories he'd heard from his mother and stepfather? He knew his father had dealt coke as well as craps, had partied and philandered. But what kind of asshole abandons his wife and child?

I was the wrong man to ask. For the last half century, I'd struggled with whether I'd abandoned my own family.

Newt thought that, one way or another, he would get together with Bryce and Carlotta Farragut Ragatz.

"When my dad disappeared, my mom asked them, his cousins, to help find him. They wouldn't. Bryce Ragatz said if Dad was alive he'd be around pretty soon, asking for money. His wife said some vicious things to my mother. That's what Merle says, anyhow."

"Your mother," I said. "Is she all right?"

"No," he said.

He spoke of her in even more carefully measured phrases. From them I took it that she'd always been odd, not cold as much as distant. She would hold the world at arm's length. Her childhood had been itinerant and impoverished, her education sporadic and incomplete. Her beauty was nearly a handicap, creating in others expectations that she was incapable of fulfilling. All but her son and her second husband had betrayed their obligation to her.

"You've thought about her a lot," I said.

"Most of this comes from Gunny," he said. "He thinks. We talk."

His mother had spent much of her life hiding behind an empty smile. To some—men mostly—this leant her an allure of mystery. Under male advances, she went blank, vacant. Then, for no reason she could ever offer, she'd married Howie Ragatz. Now she was content with her own company, her own world. She had her house, her son, and her husband, and she needed nothing and no one more. It wasn't that she disliked people, Newt said, only that she couldn't bring herself to trust them.

"She's leery. She's . . . damaged," he said. "We take care of her, Gunny and I."

I was struck again by how much, physically, he was his mother's son—the delicate features, slight frame. At the same time, as he spoke of his mother, I detected, finally, his anger. Like her, he concealed an important part of himself. Like her, he too was damaged, certainly in body, perhaps in other ways as well.

The desert hurried emptily by. Traffic coagulated around Carson City, diluted at Washoe Valley, thickened again as we approached Reno at rush hour. Off the interstate, the congestion continued, so by the time we reached the turn-off near the BLM wild horse center, the afternoon had slipped away.

Dust hung thin and still over the road on Warm Springs Mountain. The smell of scorch and char lingered in the lot of Stafford Cabinetry. As we got out, Merle Stafford stepped from his shop.

"Glad to see you." I thought he was addressing me until he added, "Your mom's been asking about you."

"Yeah," Newt said. He thanked me for the ride and started off toward the house.

Without a preface, Merle said, "So everything's out in the open now?"

"Not necessarily," I said. "Mia and Newt know each other. That's all." When he didn't respond, I went on. "I screwed up, Gunny, and she made the connection with Newt. But your wife still doesn't need to know about her."

"Yeah," he said. "How about me? Anything I ought to know about her?"

I told him what I could. "She's unhappy. Anxious. She seems to care about Newt."

He nodded, but I could tell that he was reassessing the situation. He also seemed to be assessing me: *did I too remember that I was a Marine?*

He coughed harshly. "Friend of yours stopped by. Big guy, slick, black BMW. Said he was helping you look for Howie. Said you were working for Len Maglie."

"Maglie might think so," I said. "Howie had some of his money. He wants it back."

"After all this time?" Merle Stafford looked out over the desert. Shadows darkened declivities and depressions. Soon the night creatures would be out. "What's going on, Ross?"

Merle Stafford was worried. About what I didn't know.

"I'm not sure, Gunny," I said. "But I've got a feeling we're about to find out."

Forty-five minutes later, I was pulling under my mulberry tree when my phone rang. It was the DNA lab, the technician working late because she knew how anxious Mia was to get the results of the comparison.

The samples contained no common genetic material.

Newton Ragatz and Mia Dunn were not related.

I called Mia. She'd already heard. She'd called Newt Ragatz.

I thought of calling Alicia, but what had I to tell her that she would want to hear?

SEVEN

I slept late, didn't exercise, and brooded away much of the next morning. The scene with Alicia. Frank's condition, physical and psychological. The uncertainty out on Warm Springs Mountain. Len Maglie and goons. I was, I finally realized, tipping at the edge of depression. To ease back from the dark, I got dressed and headed for Stead.

During and for some years after World War II, the small airfield in the loom of Peavine Mountain had been part of a military installation, a geometric grouping of buildings and strips of asphalt set inharmoniously on an otherwise empty desert plain. Now warehouses and tract homes surrounded runways and small hangars and businesses associated with aviation. Now the only martial presence was the Nevada Air National Guard. Peavine Mountain remained relatively unchanged, so far.

Along the main runway, BLM tankers stood as if abandoned. I made my way past them, and a glider-rental business, and a pod of small planes—Beechcraft, Cessna, and the like—to a row of hangars. The one I wanted, according to a guard at the gate, was near the end.

A silver Mercedes convertible sat before the hangar door. Two planes were parked in the dimness, an old Piper Comanche and beside it an even older, beautifully restored AD-4. A man in a mechanic's jumpsuit stood on a ladder, his arms extended, his head bent over the warplane's engine.

He looked up as I stepped into the hangar. "Be with you in a minute, Ross."

Bryce Ragatz and I had grown up in a Reno that was still a small town, and we had a small-town sort of acquaintance. He'd been three years ahead of me at Reno High, where he ran track and played basketball and I played hoops and football. We'd both been to Nam, he early and I late.

Back from the war and haunting casinos at night, I'd watched him pass through the Claim Jumper, stopping to chat with dice flingers and slot yankers. Now and then we'd have a drink and talk sports and crime and women. I hadn't been troubled by his disfigured face.

Bryce was a genuine war hero. He'd joined the navy out of UNR so that he could fly AD-4s, the relatively slow speeds of which made them effective tactical support for ground troops. In his plane he was courageous to near foolhardiness. Protecting embattled Marines, he flew low and chewed up the enemy with his guns. He also made a good target, and he became famous for returning in planes shot full of holes. He earned bronze and silver stars and a Navy Cross before finally catching an RPG. Severely burned by a spurt of hot oil over the right side of his face and neck, he managed to get his plane to water, set it down on the smooth sea, and struggle out before it sank.

That ended his war. He returned to Reno, took over a failing casino his father was about to get rid of, bought the Piper Comanche, and flew it to sites of business and pleasure around the West. He rather remarkably managed the Claim Jumper into the black. Then, at the peak of the casino-building mania in the 90s, he sold out and put his millions in high-yield bonds. To occupy his retirement, he bought and restored the AD-4, which he flew all over the country, racing, doing stunts, having fun.

I waited as he climbed down the ladder, fit a wrench into its place on a pegboard above a worktable, and wiped his hands on a greasy rag. "Got a little hiccup. Thought it was a piston, but it was just a clogged plug."

"I imagine your wife told you I'd be out to see you," I said.

"Warned me, more like it." His smile attested to masculine solidarity. She isn't totally convinced that you aren't out to cash in on one of my romps. I told her you didn't do that, but she remembered those old headlines." His smile widened. "She still isn't sure you can be trusted. You didn't take her money."

When I didn't respond, he went on easily, "This has something to do with Howie?"

I took from my pocket the photo Mia Dunn had given me. I handed it to him.

He studied it. I studied him.

As a young man he had been lean and athletic, and he was still fit, carried himself with the easy assurance of the accomplished, was one of those men who grew more attractive as he aged. His appeal was accentuated by his scar—shiny reddish skin like plastic stretched out and down from his mostly missing ear. The hot oil had splashed over his temple and cheek and neck. The pain would have been excruciating.

"Tabby Sabich," he said, nodding. "And Howie. Randy Barnes. Gale."

"Popular gal, Gale Dunn." I said. "What was the big attraction?"

He looked again at the photograph. "Hard to say, exactly. She just had . . . something."

"Randy ever connect with her?"

He frowned, the question clearly not to his liking. "I couldn't say."

"Did Howie?" When he didn't answer, I said, "Gale Dunn died a couple of months ago. Her daughter wants to know who her father was."

"Carlotta said. I hadn't heard." He unzipped and began to slip out of his jumpsuit. "She was Harvey Prior's special piece, but he'd hand her out once in a while. Barnes, he was smitten, no question, but I don't know how far it went. Harvey liked to have fun with him, embarrass him. Maybe he let him have a go at Gale, maybe not. Howie was another matter. She may have thought she was in love with him. The two of them might have had something going on. But I don't really know."

I asked an obvious question, "How about you?"

He gave me slow smile. I wasn't sure what it meant.

"About Howie," I said. "You put up the cash for his bond."

"I did," he agreed. "I liked him, and I didn't want to see him in jail." He arranged his jumpsuit on a hanger beside the workbench. Then he gave me his smile of male complicity. "I also wanted to earn the gratitude of his wife."

"I met her the other day," I said. "She's still beautiful. Back then she must have been something."

"Ah, Laurel. *Something* is the word. The question is what. Hard to tell whether she was cold or crafty or just weird." His grin wrinkled the scar tissue. "I loaned her a thousand dollars. All it bought me was an empty smile."

When he owned and managed the Claim Jumper, Bryce Ragatz had spent many of his off hours pursuing women, especially other men's wives, those married being less likely to go public or to press claims. He was said to be interested mostly in the quest, enjoyed the process of persuasion, the tension wrought by secrecy, the little thrills of slipping around—seduction, not sex, inspired him.

I wondered if he was telling me the truth about his failure with Laurel Ragatz. Or if, now, it mattered.

I changed directions. "I hear that when Howie disappeared, so did some money."

His grin faded. He stood straighter, grew more serious.

"All I know is that he really didn't want to go to prison. He needed money to hire a good lawyer, and he'd asked me for a loan. Bail was one thing, but I had to turn him down on this. It was money I didn't think I'd ever get back."

His voice, his bearing expressed his certainty.

"He said he'd pay it back soon, that he'd have plenty of cash," Ragatz said, "but I didn't believe him. He always talked about the big score. Drugs. I know he tried to work an in with Harvey, who just laughed at him. I really don't know what he was up to."

"Nobody else seems to either," I said. "The cops have come up with an interesting coincidence, though. Turns out Howie lit out, or got taken out, the same night you got robbed."

"I hadn't heard that," he said quietly. "And what do they conclude?"

"Nothing that I know of," I said. "These robbers—they got only papers, is that right?"

He nodded. "I don't know what they thought I'd have. Dumb bastards. Just routine business papers, but they cost Paulie Hauberk his hand. Maybe you've seen what a .45 can do to human flesh."

I had. I didn't want to think about it. "This Paulie, he worked for you?"

"Did little jobs for me, once in a while. He was one of Harvey's boys, at the time."

Several questions crowded into my mind. I decided to think more before I asked them. Instead, I said, "And now one of Len Maglie's."

"Maglie." Ragatz looked at me. I don't know what he saw, but it caused him to grin. "You're not going to tangle with him, are you?"

"I'm not going to tangle with anyone," I said.

"You sure? For old time's sake?" His grin spread. "The return of Jack Ross. I mean, your reputation was enough to spook Carlotta."

My reputation. Tales of another time about a man who used to be.

The phone in my pocket rang. Frank told me he was at my house, waiting for me. He had news.

Frank had parked his car under my mulberry tree. After getting a beer and putting on a CD of Pavarotti singing arias, he'd parked himself in my chair. He didn't look bad, but I could see that his high color overlay an elemental weariness. He was worn out, in decline.

I grabbed a beer, put Pavarotti on pause, and plopped onto the couch. I nodded at the manila folder that lay before him. "Don't tell me you got the robbery file?"

"I won't." He gave me his ironic sneer. "But I talked to a couple of detectives. Made some notes."

He opened the folder and removed a few neatly printed pages, which he quickly summarized for me. Basically, they repeated what he had told me before: three men in masks, an alley ambush, gunfire, a stolen brief-case, a dead Dick Pym. But there was more, I knew, or he wouldn't have been waiting for me.

"What do we know now that they didn't twenty-five years ago?"

"A little," Frank said dryly. "And maybe we know a few things a little better."

I still didn't much care who had robbed Bryce Ragatz. I could see no way the incident would be relevant to the question of Randy Barnes's marital fidelity, but I didn't say so. Frank was involved, which could only be good.

"One thing we know is how really screwy this robbery was. Who would rob a man on his way *in* to a casino? On the way *out*, maybe. What the hell did these guys think they'd get?"

"I don't know," I said. "Dope?"

"There was never any suggestion that Ragatz had anything to do with the dope business."

"Harvey Prior did."

Frank paused. Bryce Ragatz had frequented Prior's club. Prior had gambled at Ragatz's casino. Officials had looked for other connections but had found nothing. Prior's dancers were not to Ragatz's taste, word was, and Ragatz's crap tables were neither generous nor niggardly when Prior had the dice. The two men professed to be old friends, Harvey Prior having from time to time done little jobs for Bryce Ragatz's father. Pressed, Ragatz would not deny the relationship. Some people in town thought his loyalty admirable.

"Nobody ever linked him to any of Prior's activities, no matter how hard they tried."

I knew that. "Where does that leave you?"

He tried his beer. "It leaves me wondering—about Joe Kohler's alibi, for instance."

That July Friday night, the streets of downtown Reno had echoed with the reverberations of motorcycle engines, bikers having descended on the city to fuss and bluster. Many were in and out of Roscoe's, a dive a cou-ple of blocks from the Claim Jumper. Joe Kohler was there too, drinking boilermakers until he got into a violent altercation with a man wearing the colors of the Branded Few. Chaos and havoc ensued, continuing until a phalanx of cops arrived. Kohler, cheekbone broken and rib cracked, ended up in jail after a trip to St. Mary's ER.

"Witnesses—those they could identify and find—put him in the bar when the robbery was going down," Frank said, "but everyone was in and out, and bombed or stoned or both, and no one could swear that Kohler had been there every minute. He'd have had plenty of opportunity to slip out, do the deed, and get back. Who would know he was gone? Or care?"

"This is what detectives think now?"

"It's what *I* think," he said. "It's possible, that's all I'm saying. Somebody should ask Mr. Kohler a few questions. While he's at it, that somebody should talk to the guy who got shot."

I remembered the questions I hadn't asked Bryce Ragatz. What was Prior's goon, the square man, doing with the casino owner that evening? Why was he packing? Was he driver, bodyguard, what?

"Feel free," I said.

Frank drained his beer. "You don't think it's worth bracing them?"

"It would be," I said, "if I cared. But I don't."

"Why not?"

"I'm retired," I said. "I don't do this kind of thing anymore. I'm just trying to help your sister."

He didn't respond. Then, as over the years we had come often to do, Frank and I settled into silence. What, after so long a friendship, had we to say?

I got up and let Pavarotti sing to us again. Frank closed his eyes, listening. Stilled, he looked like a dead man.

Just talking, thinking, had worn him down. He seemed reduced, in both flesh and spirit. He was interested for the moment in an old botched robbery, but he would soon tire of pondering it as, since he'd lost Sheila, he had tired of nearly everything.

I had a sudden vision of Paltry, less scarecrow than Grim Reaper, standing watch over a garden in which nothing grew.

A gout of emotion—affection, foreboding, sorrow—swelled heavily in my chest. Frank was my friend, my only friend, really. When he went, I would be, in a way that I hadn't been for nearly sixty years, alone.

Frank and I had lunch at the Gold and Silver, then parted, he to return home to stand watch with Paltry, me to do what I didn't do anymore.

A short while later, I idled down a dusty street bordered by half-dead elms in a quietly deteriorating Sparks neighborhood of pre-World War II bungalows of various size and design. A few homes had trimmed lawns, bright paint, and other indications of the owner-occupied, but most were rentals fronted by crumbling concrete walks and oil-stained dirt, by steps and porches out of square, by the appurtenances of neglect.

The house I wanted was a beat-up brown clapboard. Half the lawn was littered with junked automobile pieces and parts, half was wet from some subterranean source. Drapes blinded windows on either side of the door, from which slanted a ramp spotted with bird droppings. On the roof, wooden shingles curled and cracked.

I parked, negotiated the ramp, and knocked. No one answered. In a battered mailbox I found fliers addressed to Joe and to Rollo Kohler. I made my way around to the back, where a huge old cherry tree loomed leafless over more car parts and tools covered in weather-hardened grime. At the back of the house was a small elevated porch on which, in a wheelchair parked in the sun, sat a human wreck, seeking heat.

"Joe Kohler?"

He had been a big man. Now, nearly fleshless, he was mostly twisted bone and swollen joint. His spotted skull was hairless, his mouth slack. From his pajama bottoms extended ankles like tree knots. His feet were lumpy and twisted in his slippers.

I climbed the four steps up to the porch. Closer, I could see that he wasn't as old as I'd first thought—sixty or thereabouts. His pupils were dilated by drugs, opiates for pain, probably.

He lifted a gnarled hand, dark with a smear of old jailhouse tattoos, as if to shade his eyes. His mouth moved, words coming with effort. "I know you?"

"I'm asking folks about Howie Ragatz," I said. "Your name keeps coming up."

Red blotches appeared at his throat. "Fuck you."

I smiled. "No thanks."

"I'd kick your ass." He again raised and now examined his ugly diseased hand, much as Len Maglie had admired his own fist. "Fucking arthur-ritis got me."

His ass-kicking days were clearly past. He lived now in doped-up, dull-minded pain. I felt no sympathy. "I hear you mostly frightened women. Like Laurel Ragatz."

"Snooty cunt." He shook his head, wincing. "She knows about my money."

That got my attention. "What money?"

"The money you're looking for," he said. "Why else would anybody be asking about Howie Ragatz after all this time?"

"What money?" I repeated.

He stiffened under a serious pain. "He had it. Then he was gone, and the money with him. She killed him, her and that Stafford asshole—that's what I figured."

He didn't need encouragement to tell me, slowly, nearly every other word an obscenity, what he'd figured. He frowned at small pains, grimaced stiffly at those that momentarily took away his breath.

At first, he'd thought that Laurel Ragatz and Merle Stafford had killed her husband and taken the cash he'd been holding. Kohler had pressured them but they didn't fold. So he waited, watching them, but they spent no money they couldn't account for. Then he began to think that Harvey Prior might have murdered Howie, that he had tried to buy his way into a major drug deal and Prior had Len Maglie kill him and take the money. Or maybe it was jealousy—Howie was always sniffing around that dancer Prior had staked a claim on. But Maglie was looking for Howie too, even after Prior was gone. Finally, Kohler concluded that Howie Ragatz had taken the money and run.

Telling me this took him a while and depleted his energy. His head sagged, chin nearly to chest. He twisted in pain.

"If Prior'd killed him, there'd of been a body. They'd dump him in the middle of Victorian Square, let everybody see what happens to guys who fucked with Harvey Prior."

"The money," I said. "Where'd it come from?"

He gave me a look, a grotesque parody of cunning. "Find it for me, and I'll tell you."

"How much money are we talking about?" I asked.

"My share—eighty, ninety grand," he said.

"Your share—that's half, a third, fourth, what?"

He tried to smile but gave up the effort. "Whatever."

I wasn't going to get much this way. "Len Maglie says the money belongs to him."

"Fuck him." But his face had changed. He wanted no part of Len Maglie.

"The dancer," I tossed out. "Gale Dunn."

"Figured her for it too, for a while." He spoke even more slowly. He was exhausted. "If Howie'd run, she might follow. Never did."

I took a different tack. "If you were looking for the money now, where would you start?"

As if he hadn't heard me, he said, "Bitch. She called me a while back, drunk, said the wife and boyfriend killed Howie, said if I'd kill them I could have the money. All of it."

Drunk and alone, Gale Dunn had sent her paranoia into the night. "What did you do?"

Again he looked at his hand. "What could I, like this? Nothing for a long time. Then finally I sent them a message."

I didn't know what that last meant, for certain, but it didn't matter.

"Snooty bitch. She'll get hers yet."

Laurel Stafford, he meant. "You're in no shape to give anybody anything."

His face went red with rage. "I want my fucking money! I need it. I fucking hurt!"

"It's been over twenty years," I said. "Any money in this is long gone."

To that he had nothing more to say. Neither did I. I left him there.

I WAS EASING around the muddy patch of lawn when a red Chevy crew cab hurtled down the street and slammed to a stop. The man who got out was young, in his mid-twenties, and very large. His head was shaved and his beard bushy. Massive tallowed and tattooed arms jutted from his sleeveless camouflage shirt. A heavy gut hung over his belt.

"You looking for me?" His snarl was practiced.

I shook my head. "Nope."

"You sure? Rollo Kohler?" When I didn't answer, he stepped onto the walk, blocking my passage. He leaned his bulk at me. "You ain't P and P? Who the fuck are you then? What are you doing, sneaking around my house?"

He irritated me, the look of him, the greasy shine of his pate. But I just said, "I've been having a little chat with Joe."

"Gramps? Chat about what?"

"That would be between him and me," I said.

"You're trespassing, motherfucker." His anger, I saw, was feigned. He was having fun, a bully blustering before what he thought was weakness.

"If you'll stand aside, I'll be happy to get off your property," I said.

He didn't step aside. He stepped ahead. "I could make a citizen's arrest. You could try to resist. Old fucker like you, you could get hurt real bad."

His breath smelled of pizza and beer. His pores, especially around his nose, gaped. His eyes were a curious, almost beautiful blue.

I didn't like him in my face, but I didn't move. "I wouldn't care for that," I said.

He put a thick hand on my chest, shoved, lightly.

I didn't move.

He shoved harder.

I'd thought he was just messing with me. Now I wasn't so sure.

He was young and, despite the gut and flab, probably strong. I guessed that he depended on his size and had never learned to fight. But if he got his hands on me, he'd hurt me.

Still, all I had to do was step around him, get in my car, and drive away. I couldn't manage it. Old impulses flickered, flared.

"Careful, sonny," I said quietly.

He stared at me, beginning to understand that I wasn't afraid of him. He seemed insulted. His shoulders stiffened as his anger grew real. With an animal growl, he reached for me.

I slipped under his grasp and moved away, backing slowly onto the edge of the yard.

When he charged me, I stepped around him and shoved. He slipped, ended up on his back in the middle of the muddy patch of lawn.

I watched him get up. I was breathing deeply, less from actual exertion than from apprehension. And age. I was too old for this nonsense.

I said, "Why don't we pack it in before one of us gets hurt?"

Patches of red appeared on his shaved pate. He was so angry now that he seemed no longer to see. From a half crouch he threw himself at me.

Hot, tired, old, and suddenly angry myself, I did something really stupid. I hit him.

I hit him with my fist, my right, as hard as I could, but as I aimed at his chin, he dipped his head, and the blow caught him in the middle of his forehead.

Pain flamed in my hand, surged into my wrist and forearm, coursed up into my shoulder. The hand was broken, I knew immediately. I knew too that I'd made a big mistake.

Rollo Kohler had gone down, toppled onto his side. He was stunned, but he recovered quickly and crawled to his feet. Mud smeared the side of his head, ear, clumped in his beard.

He saw that I was hurt, cradling my right hand in my left. His grin exposed big yellow teeth. "You're finished now, old man."

He wasn't good, but he was young and strong and could wear me down. I had to get this over with, and fast.

Wary now, he eased toward me. He was red with heat and effort, sweating, odiferous. I let him get close. When he reached for me, I stiffened the fingers of my good hand and jabbed him hard in the larynx.

His eyes went wide as his hands clutched at his throat. He made a sound, a faint, painful squawk. He sat in the muddy grass.

I left him there. Moving around my Subaru, I noticed, half a block away, a man leaning against the fender of a white SUV. The square man. The one-handed man.

I walked over. "Paulie, wasn't it?"

He looked at me without expression.

"I'm headed for the Renown Emergency Room, then home, if you're tailing me. You can tag along if you want, but I'd think Maglie might have better things for you to do."

His face didn't change. "I'll stick. Might get to see more amateur-hour stuff."

"You'll be old one of these days," I said.

"Didn't mean you," he said. He held up the black rubber stub of his arm. "Looks like you're one-handed too. That was a nice move there at the end, though. Old army trick?"

"Marines," I said.

On the lawn, Rollo Kohler put out a hand and pushed himself up from the mud. His other hand remained at his throat. He looked over at us. He was red with rage and pain.

I would see him again, I assumed. He'd want to hurt me.

"He'll have fun eating," Paulie said. "Talking too. Croak like a fucking frog."

My hand throbbed. It had begun to swell, to take on sickly color. My head hurt too, from the adrenaline. I fought off a wave of nausea. I needed help.

Then, without actually thinking about it, I asked, "What were you doing with Bryce Ragatz the night you got your hand shot off?"

He looked at me. "Been busy, haven't you."

I shrugged. "Just doing a favor for Len Maglie."

"And I was just following orders," he said, one grunt to another. "Like always."

By nightfall I was home, stuffed with Tylenol, once again in my chair, again watching the night. My hand still pained, but not as much. On it I wore a two-fingered, glove-like splint, which I'd need for a couple weeks, at least. A Brawler's Fracture, the ER doctor told me, broken necks of the fourth and fifth metacarpals. Boxer's Fracture, he said it was called as well. I thought a better term was Fool's Fracture.

I'd acted impulsively, getting after Joe Kohler. I didn't know what, if anything, I'd learned that might be important.

I didn't know why I'd gone angry and stupid with Rollo Kohler, who, ugly piece of work that he was, would now be looking for payback.

I didn't know why I'd broken into Mia Dunn's apartment the day before. I didn't know what was happening to me.

The only thing I had left to do was talk to Tabby Sabich, but I wasn't up to it.

I stayed put, made a meal, listened to Benny Goodman play Mozart.

My nerves were too jangled for sleep. Eventually I took up *The Troubled Man*, the final novel of Henning Mankell, dead a month earlier. Pain pills and Scandinavian gloom got me to sleep, finally, at midnight.

EIGHT

Nine hours later, I was settled in a chair at a small desk in a corner at the Veterans' Outreach Office, prepared to listen.

For several years I had rotated with other volunteers providing legal information to vets who had questions or problems. Every third Friday I listened to men and women, many sound enough physically and emotionally, but others bruised or broken by war, some who felt used and abandoned by their country. To these few, I attended as they recounted fantasies and dreams and nightmares, told elaborate lies and confused tales about drugs, alcohol, sex, love, violence, bad luck, and bad choices, frustration, madness, dread.

I didn't presume to counsel, leaving that to those who decades earlier had counseled me. I explained rights and listed legal options, made referrals, phoned and wrote letters and sent emails. And I listened.

Today I fielded only a couple of inquiries—a child-custody matter, an eviction. That gave me time to think about my promise to Alicia. I wasn't much closer to answering her question about Randy than I'd been when she asked it. All I had to show for a search of several days were bits of fact, surmise, guess, and two dully aching broken bones in my hand.

When it was clear that no one else was going to want me to listen to them today, I did a quick computer search for Rollo Kohler. He'd done jail time but managed to stay out of prison, just barely. Both Sparks and Washoe County had run him in, on charges ranging from auto theft to assault, but they couldn't get anything to stick. He was thought to do little jobs for his grandfather.

I thought I knew now who had set fire to Merle Stafford's barn, and why.

What it meant was another question. Still, I couldn't see how most of it related to my only real interest.

Howie Ragatz was not Mia Dunn's father. That left Harvey Prior, Bryce Ragatz, and Randy Barnes as candidates, plus whomever Prior might have had Gale Dunn service. Those I couldn't check out, and Harvey Prior was dead, his family scattered, and while Bryce Ragatz probably didn't care if he had fathered Gale Dunn's child, his wife no doubt did and would see that he provided no DNA to anyone. Which left Randy Barnes.

Who, I again told myself, was the only object of Alicia's concern. And mine. I would help Mia Dunn, but my primary obligation was to establish Randy's fidelity. Or lapse therefrom.

To that end, before I left at noon I called Alicia. She didn't answer. I recorded a message reminding her to search Randy's home office for something that might hold his DNA.

I called Frank too. No answer. That troubled me a bit. I decided to swing by his house after I finished doing what I was about to do.

Not much later I parked in a visitor's space at Lemon Tree Apartments. The place was a surprise, well-built and -maintained, in California Mission style—terra cotta and real adobe, bougainvillea, citrus trees and cacti and yucca in heavy clay pots, and neat strips of lush if now autumn-yellowed lawn, all arranged around a good-sized pool carefully covered by a gray tarp.

A small arrowed sign directed me to the manager's office. I pressed the button beside the door and, waiting, watched as down the walkway sauntered two young women, one of whom I'd seen selecting CDs in Len Maglie's club.

I pressed the button again. The woman who opened the door filled it. A brightly colored muumuu made her body mere mass. Fat overwhelmed her features. Glittery cat's-eye glasses framed her suspicious squint. Tabby Sabich.

I told her who I was, gave her a card.

"Pretty old for this game," she scoffed. "Can you still get it up?"

I gave her what I hoped was a friendly smile. "Not much call for it these days."

She nodded at my splinted hand, "Taking care of yourself, were you?"

I smiled again. "At my age it's way too much work."

"You're Ross." She assessed me. She'd handled better, her sneer said. "They said you'd probably show up. I'm supposed to talk to you. I don't know why. I got nothing to tell anybody about Howie Ragatz."

"What about Gale Dunn?"

"Yeah, her kid said she'd passed." She seemed unmoved. "We were roomies, years ago. What about her?"

At that moment another young woman, this one in a few inches of skirt and a blouse full of bust, tottered down the walk on high spiked heels.

"May I come in?" I smiled again. "I feel like a Bible salesman at a bordello out here."

She didn't quite laugh. We stood there. Finally, she stepped aside, into a small office: counter and cabinet, desk and appropriate devices. Hesitantly, as if hobbled, she led me into a large room dominated by a stuffed couch-and-chairs set covered in plush pastels, their backs adorned with antimacassars and fat cloth cats. A coffee table held a slew of magazines that celebrated the antics of celebrities and personalities. The only things that didn't fit were three Max Brand paperbacks stacked on a lamp table beside a large Barcalounger.

She lowered herself into a chair from which she could both watch the flat television on one wall and look out a window into the pool area. Another wall was covered with photos—old Polaroids, small snaps and glossy black-and-whites, several set pieces and a few formal shots in color. All fixed Tabitha Sabich, decades and pounds earlier, in various poses and costumes and stages of undress.

She noticed me noticing. She glared, as if I were responsible for the story the photos seemed to tell. "I didn't always look like this. I was a dancer, an artist."

"Yes, I know," I said. I let that register with her. "I have a photograph too."

I took out the shot that Mia Dunn had sent to Alicia. Tabby Sabich gave it a glance. "Those were the days, huh?"

She shifted in her chair. The movement exposed a swollen white ankle. Her slippered foot looked twisted, painfully.

"For us all," I said. Then I went on quickly, surmising, "Len Maglie owns these apartments?"

"Snooks Hale is in charge, it was his idea," she said, "but yeah, Len owns it. I manage the place, rent the units, see to the upkeep, ride herd on the entertainers that live here. They're always partying, or falling for a smile or a fat wallet, or deciding they're due more or better, or getting strung out."

"Or pregnant," I said.

"Not very often," she said harshly. "And not for long."

"Unlike Gale."

She looked again at the photograph. "Her kid doesn't look anything like her, does she?"

"Must take after her father," I said.

"That's really what you're up to? Trying to find out who knocked Gale up?" Her mouth puffed into a pout. "Line forms at the end."

"So I hear. But I don't get it," I said, holding up the photo. "She was attractive enough, I guess, but so were you. I can't see what was so special about her."

She looked again at the past. "I don't know. She wasn't that great a dancer. I mean, technically, she never had any training, she didn't . . . but she was like that song." Envy, even after all these years, tightened her voice. "That Beatles song, the one about something in the way she moves. That one."

I wasn't sure I understood, but it didn't matter. I asked more questions, and Tabby Sabich gave me answers, some forthright, some rueful, some drenched in the disgust that worn-out women have for all but a very few men. A sort of story emerged.

How Gale Dunn ended up dancing at the Blue Flame Tabby didn't know. The usual way, she supposed—it didn't matter. What mattered was that men crowded the club to see her: she appealed physically, sexually. What also mattered was that from the moment she walked into the club, she was Harvey Prior's. Oh, sure, she still had to grind it out with the pole or on laps, she still hustled, she still went with men who could give Prior a reason to share her. But he took her on trips, to parties. He bought her trinkets. She was his, and everybody knew it. Then along came Howie Ragatz.

How Gale Dunn and Howie Ragatz got together Tabby didn't know either. When Gale danced, Howie sat and watched and smiled his little smile. And then, somehow, they were getting it on. Not that anybody knew it, for sure, although Tabby had seen them in suspect circumstances. They were careful, but there were signs. There were rumors.

Then all kinds of things happened, almost, it seemed, at once. Gale Dunn got pregnant. Howie Ragatz disappeared. Harvey Prior lit out for Arizona. Len Maglie took over. Gale Dunn had her child and took her back to her parents and the Gardnerville alfalfa farm.

I had a thought, a question. "Why did she go on with the pregnancy?"

"She wanted out," the fat woman said. "Can't dance when you're pregnant, can you? And after you have a kid, you go saggy. Besides, once Howie lit out, she started hating everybody, drinking, getting mean."

At the same time that she discovered she carried death in her head. But I didn't say so. Instead I asked, "Is that what he did? Howie? Lit out?"

She shrugged her thick, colorfully clad shoulder. "Gale didn't think so. Twenty-five years later, she's calling me, drunk, crying about how he'd never have left her and somebody must have killed him and all that."

"You went to Gardnerville to see her a few of times."

"Spying," she said. "He—Maglie—thought she might be in touch with Howie. She wasn't."

"Who do you think fathered her child?" At her shrug, I tossed out names, among them Bryce Ragatz and Randy Barnes.

The casino owner used to hang around the club, she said, but although he had a yen for Gale—who didn't? —he wasn't really interested in the sort of woman who worked at the Blue Flame. He went there for a drink and a little amusement.

Randy Barnes she remembered with a sneer. He was hopeless about Gale, hopeless and stupid. He wanted to help her. He wanted to get her out of the club. And he wanted to get her away from Howie Ragatz, a married man who could only give her grief.

She looked again at the photograph I'd shown her. "They weren't always so chummy, those two. They had a couple of set-tos. Over Gale. And money—I never did know what that was about. But I know Barnes wasn't unhappy when Howie disappeared."

I looked at the photograph, at Howie Ragatz's satisfied smile, Randy Barnes's stupefied grin. "Are you telling me that Randal Barnes might have killed Howie Ragatz?"

She shrugged. "You're the private detective. You figure it out."

"I'll try." I rose. "Thank you. I know Maglie told you to talk to me, but you've given me more than you had to. I appreciate it."

She seemed surprised.

"I'm sorry I never got to see you dance."

"Me too," she said. "Me too."

I showed myself out.

As I opened my car door, my phone rang. Alicia's voice was raspy, almost gruff, as if she spoke through gritted teeth. "Can you come over, Jack? Please?"

Alicia had never before invited me to her home.

"Be right there," I said.

Even contending with rush-hour traffic, I made it fairly quickly to McCarran and then the turn-off into Caughlin Ranch.

Thirty years ago, the lanes winding over the foothill property of an erstwhile cattle operation bore some of Reno's more fashionable addresses. Since then, newer upscale developments had siphoned off some of the Caughlin Ranch cachet, but the neighborhood still had status, many of the homes selling for seven figures.

The house Alicia and Randy Barnes had shared spread over a desert slope xeriscaped with shrubs and native grasses. The building was constructed of local rust-colored rock and dark wood and pale plaster, with wide windows and redwood decks looking out onto a small reedy pond and, in the distance, the urban mess of Reno and Sparks. The view at night would be spectacular.

The front door opened before I reached it. Alicia stared at my hand. "What happened?"

I shrugged. "Old bones."

"Old bones," she echoed.

She sipped from a glass of ice and clear liquid. Her brow furrowed as if she might be confused, even pained. Her makeup was perfect, but her eyes were watery, and lipstick stained her glass. The tail of her beige blouse was hanging out. This drink wasn't her first.

I was surprised. Alicia had never been much for the booze. She was clearly upset.

We went in. Like her person, her home was carefully decorated, glossy wood and quiet cloth and local art. Wide archways led to spacious rooms with good furniture arranged to allow intimate groupings, to enable entertaining rather than living. With its cathedral ceilings and large windows, the living room might have passed for the empty lobby of a five-star resort hotel.

Alicia silently and a bit unsteadily led me to a smaller doorway into what almost seemed another residence, an antechamber off which opened a kitchen, a short hallway leading to a utility room and the garage, and another hallway with two closed doors. She opened one of these and showed me into a cramped office, desk and chair and cabinet and book shelves, an old leather couch, a small safe. All was tidy, dustless, smelling faintly of lemon.

"There was nothing that would have his DNA," Alicia said. "After he died I gave everything to St. Vincent's and I—the service cleans in here every week, even though I hardly ever come in." She took another sip of her drink. "But there's that."

On the desk lay an unmarked manila folder. Alicia looked at it as if afraid to touch it. "I—I don't know what it is."

She'd found it, she said, in the safe. Anxiously she added, "I didn't want Frank to see it. Otherwise, I would have . . . but I couldn't think of anyone else to call."

The folder contained a thick sheaf of papers, carefully clipped together, and a letter. The papers had to do with financial transactions—stock sales and purchases, cash transfers and fund adjustments, account openings and closings, the manipulation of large and small sums of the money of Bryce Ragatz. The letter was a copy of the one sent to Mia Dunn by a Wells Fargo vice-president telling her that she should close out the trust account established to help pay for her education.

Alicia emptied her drink. "What is it, Jack? What does it mean?"

"I'm not sure," I said. "This may take a while."

I sat, bent to it. When I finally looked up, Alicia was perched stiffly on the old couch. She again emptied her glass.

"Randy did work for Bryce Ragatz," I said. "We knew that. This is a record of his moving money around, apparently to reduce Ragatz's taxes."

She nodded impatiently. "But . . . the letter?"

"I'd guess that Bryce had Randy put money in trust for Mia Dunn's education," I said. "I mean, there's no direct evidence of that, and I suppose the letter could have just been misfiled, but that's what it looks like, that Randy worked with the bank, acting on Ragatz's behalf. Bryce could confirm it. But . . . "

Something didn't quite add up. I didn't know enough about tax law to understand what it was—maybe just a very sophisticated set of negotiations that let Bryce Ragatz take advantage of loopholes. Maybe.

"I need to study this. I might have to talk to a forensic accountant." I leaned back in the chair. "It's Friday, no one will be available till Monday. Can I take this file with me?"

"Monday," she repeated, flushing, frustrated. "Why is this all taking so long, Jack? What have you been doing? You said there was DNA from that man's, from Howie Ragatz's son. You said Howie Ragatz was the girl's father."

I hadn't said that, but I didn't argue. "It turns out not. DNA says there's no connection. But the whole thing is more complicated than we thought."

I told her about Len Maglie and his minions, about the robbery of Bryce Ragatz, about Newt Ragatz and his mother, about Rollo and Joe Kohler, about Gale Dunn.

Through this, Alicia stared into her empty glass. I wasn't sure she was listening.

When I finished, she looked up. "It's all so ugly. It's like all that nastiness you used to be involved in all the time."

I prepared to object, then didn't. Maybe she was right. Maybe that was why I was subject to old urges. Why I was teetering toward depression.

Alicia wasn't finished. "But most of it doesn't really matter, does it? To me, I mean. So now you think it was, the father was . . . who? Bryce Ragatz?"

I shook my head. "I don't know. He did a lot of bed-hopping, but not with strippers. He preferred wives, word was."

"Word was. Vicious gossip." She flushed again, now in anger. "Have you . . . What have you heard?"

It was less a question than an implicit refutation.

"About Bryce," I said, "nothing new. Nothing relevant. Except now, this file—why would Bryce Ragatz provide for Gale Dunn's daughter? There's an obvious answer, isn't there?"

The color faded from her throat. "And Randy? Is there any . . . ?"

"No," I said, "I haven't met a single soul who says that Randy ever cheated on you, with Gale Dunn or anybody else."

I thought about telling her what Tabby Sabich had just told me, but I decided not to. I wouldn't lie to her, but neither would I tell her anything I wasn't certain of.

She looked at me, seemed to try to look into me. As I had in the bistro, I sensed that she wanted to say something. But then her gaze changed.

She swayed and raised her empty glass. "I got scared. I thought this would help. It didn't."

I could guess what had frightened her. The file connected her husband to money and Mia Dunn. "Is there anything I can do?"

"No, I'm fine," she said. "I'll take some coffee and a bit of pâté out onto the deck and enjoy the end of the day. I'll be all right."

I rose, took up the file. "I'll get back to you as soon as I can."

She looked at me again. "I'm sorry about the other day."

"Me too," I said.

She closed her eyes for a moment. Then she said, "Whatever possessed us, Jack? To marry, I mean?"

Possessed seemed exactly the right word. At least in my case. But I didn't say so.

She rose. She thanked me for coming over. She showed me out.

Three hours later, at my office desk, I again looked up from the Ragatz file. I still didn't understand what Randy had been doing. Transaction by transaction, everything seemed simple enough, but taken together the various moves constituted a maze. My attempts to follow the movement of money invariably ended in futility.

But maybe I just didn't get it. My knowledge of accounting practices was rudimentary. And I wasn't at my best. I was tired, and distracted—the day had been long, and my meeting with Alicia again disturbing.

I put away the file, found a beer, and listened to the Beatles harmonize the lyric Tabby Sabich thought described Gale Dunn and her powerful appeal.

Gale Dunn was dead. I would never know what exactly it was about her that moved so many men. But I had an inkling of how they were affected.

No one had ever attracted me like Alicia Calvetti. One day she was my friend Frank's sullen pretty sister, the next the dark-eyed, soft-mouthed object of an urging elemental and essentially mindless. As we moved from awkward courtship to intense honeymoon, I would have said that I thought about little else but Alicia, but in fact I hardly thought of her at all. I wanted.

Fifty years later, I could still remember, could almost again feel the force of old desire, the body's betrayal, the blood's yearning. How could it not drive us to disaster, this mindlessness?

NINE

The wind shivered the sagebrush as I ran. A front was approaching, bringing snow to the Sierra and, if we were lucky, some rain to the Truckee Meadows. Meanwhile, gusts threatened my balance, and my hand pained me, so I cut short the jog.

At home, clean and fed, I gave Frank a call. I had forgotten, the evening before, that I'd planned to stop by. Now he sounded tired, his voice hollow. I told him I'd look in on him later.

Then I took coffee and the manila file Alicia had given me out to the patio, where I sat in the sun and again tried to make out what Randy Barnes had been doing with Bryce Ragatz's money. All of the dealings were documented, everything appeared aboveboard, but some seemed purposeless, accounts opened and closed for no reason, deposits swallowed, penalties paid, options exercised, assets shifted.

Time passed. The blustery wind shook the screen door, rattled the loose lid of an old metal garbage can at the back of the house. I read and puzzled over the manipulation of money until I was startled by the slide of the opening screen door. Snooks Hale, again in black, looked around. Assured that I was alone, he stepped aside to usher out Len Maglie, elegantly attired and appointed.

I closed the file and stood up.

Maglie smiled as he approached, his voice a rumble. "Heard about your set-to with the big boy, Ross. Dumb. Guys our age don't want to be banging on bone. Go for soft tissue."

His smile brightened as he lifted his right hand, clenched in a fist. Then he hooked his other fist into my liver.

I collapsed onto the patio brick, aware as if from a great distance that I was on my hands and knees and in trouble. I hurt. I could see only smears, couldn't move my legs. I heaved violently, at once gagging and gasping for air.

Maglie left me to recover, slowly. Eventually I struggled up, wobbly, sick with pain, and crawled into a chair.

The two men were seated in the sunlight. Snooks watched me coolly. Maglie was leafing through the manila file. "What's this got to do with Howie Ragatz?"

I managed to make a word. "Nothing."

He lifted the file, opened it, and let the papers in it flutter to the patio. "You haven't been doing what I told you to do, Ross. Just fussing with kids, fighting fat guys, pestering my people. You think I was fucking kidding, did you?"

"A fool's errand," I said slowly.

"You calling me a fool?" His voice had deepened. "I thought you said you wasn't crazy anymore."

"I'm the fool," I said, "getting suckered like that."

"Yeah," he said, "You ain't much anymore, Ross. If you ever were."

I tried to gather myself, to control my body. And my anger. "You want me to find Howie Ragatz and some money, but you don't tell me what I need to know to do it."

A paper from the file skittered across the patio on a small squall of wind. Maglie watched it, frowning. "Like what?"

I gave it to him in pieces, as my retching reflex stilled and my breathing settled.

I needed to know about money. How much money? Where did it come from? How did Howie Ragatz get it? Maglie said it was his, but Joe Kohler also claimed it. Howie disappeared the day Bryce Ragatz was robbed, and some cops thought now that Howie and Kohler may have been the other two with Dick Pym in masks, but Bryce Ragatz said that the robbers got only business papers. So what kind of papers were so valuable that he had to be protected by an armed Paulie Hauberk—Paulie, now Maglie's muscle, who then worked for Harvey Prior? What were Bryce Ragatz and Harvey Prior up to? And maybe Howie Ragatz ran off with the money, but if not, then somebody killed him. But did they kill him for the money or for some other reason? Who had cause to do him harm? And Howie Ragatz hadn't been seen in twenty-five years, and all of a sudden people are looking for him and some money. Why?

Len Maglie scowled silently. The wind eddied. Papers trembled, floated, slid.

"Howie wasn't the father of Gale Dunn's daughter," I added. "All I want is to find out who was, so a young nurse can know who she is."

"Sounds like you've been doing something after all." Maglie again held up and admired his fist. "So I'll tell you. The money was mine—a quarter of a million, from a business deal that fell through. If Joe fucking Kohler claims otherwise, he can take it up with me. Howie was just a delivery boy. And you want to know about Bryce Ragatz and Harvey Prior? Harvey sold dope. Bryce Ragatz flew a plane. You figure it out. The robbery—read the police report. Paulie was driving because Bryce was bombed, and he was armed because he always is, licensed and legal. Other than that, who cares, except maybe Paulie'd like to know for sure who shot off his hand. If Bryce Ragatz says they didn't get anything, they didn't get anything. Leave it be."

I'd come back to myself, anger gone cold. I wasn't inclined to believe anything Len Maglie had said, although the Bryce Ragatz-Harvey Prior connection made a certain kind of shocking sense. The only thing I'd learned was that Len Maglie knew Joe fucking Kohler.

"What if Howie's disappearance had nothing to do with money or drugs? Who had reason to want him dead?"

Maglie smiled. "Yeah, who? Snooks, who might have had a hard-on for old Howie?"

"That would have been the fellow whose widow happens to be Ross's ex-wife."

Tabby Sabich had told me the same thing.

"You been lying to me, Ross." Maglie grinned now, as if exceedingly pleased. "You want to know about the money man."

He reached in his jacket pocket and withdrew a photograph and slid it over to me. Randy Barnes in a hot tub, the same redwood bowl Howie Ragatz occupied in the photo Mia Dunn had found. Randy's smile was at once eager and abashed as he watched Gale Dunn, wearing only a bikini bottom, step into the water.

"Paulie says you spent a lot of time with Barnes's widow the last couple days. Turns out she's your ex. She's the one you're doing a favor for, ain't she. The little girl wants to know who's her daddy, but ex wants to know was it hubby."

"Alicia Barnes isn't involved in this," I said. "She and I are talking because we're concerned about her brother, my friend. He's not well."

Maglie laughed, a scoffing snort, and tapped a finger on the photograph. "Yeah, right. That means it's okay if I show this to her." When I didn't reply, he grinned. "Thought so."

I felt my anger heating again.

"You can have that," Maglie said, "I got others—Harvey's way of keeping some guys in line. He had a whole cabinet full of this kind of shit."

He rose. "Here's the deal, Ross. Find Howie or the money, or tell me what happened to them, I give you what Harvey had on Burns. You don't, I give it all to the widow."

"Barnes," I said. "His name was Randal Barnes."

He ignored that. He looked out over the roofs and treetops of the city. "Tell you what. Find me Howie Ragatz and I'll give you a bonus. I'll tell you who knocked up Gale Dunn."

Snooks led his boss into the house. Soon, out front an automobile engine coughed. Then Snooks again stood in my patio doorway. He smiled. "I don't mind banging on the bones of old men. Old women either."

I had nothing to say to that.

"The robbery Len says nobody cares about. I might care about it. If you figure it out."

Then he was gone.

For a while I didn't move. At last, slowly, aching, still at the edge of nausea, I hobbled about retrieving the Ragatz file papers, several of which had blown into my front yard. I took them inside and sat in my chair and put them back in order. Then I simply sat, for a long time, thinking of nothing. And then I saw it.

I took up the file again, read through it with rising certainty. I'd still need confirmation from a forensic accountant, but I was sure.

I looked at the photograph of Randy Barnes and Gale Dunn. The more I learned about Randy, the less well I knew him.

The ache in my liver dulled to soreness. I got up and, moving, felt a bit better. I drank a cup of coffee, scrambled and ate a couple of eggs, and was about to return to my chair and the file when my phone rang.

The desk sergeant at the Sparks Police Department asked if I might come over. There had been an incident. Detectives had a few questions for me.

I knew better than to ask for additional information. I said I'd be there shortly.

AN OVERCAST GRAYED the evening sky by the time I stepped out of the East Prater Way complex. The detectives had done their jobs, I'd done mine. They'd posed careful questions, which I answered with equal care. They often repeated and rephrased their inquiries. I gave unvaried responses. They urged elaboration. I volunteered nothing. By the time they finally let me go, I'd learned from them nearly as much as they had from me, which wasn't very much at all.

Joe Kohler was dead. He'd been savaged by a tire iron, which had broken bones in his skull and face and neck. An autopsy would determine which blow actually killed him.

A crime of passion, the detectives allowed. Spontaneous, probably, the murder weapon at hand amid the junk strewn over his yard under the huge cherry tree.

What, a detective abruptly asked, had Joe Kohler done or said that had so enraged me that I grabbed the tire iron and beat him to death? I said that I hadn't done that.

He'd died Friday night between seven, when his grandson, Rollo Kohler, had gone out for beer and burgers, and his return at ten, when he discovered the body.

I'd spent those hours at home, alone. A detective made a show of writing that down.

The detectives used a great deal of energy and ingenuity questioning me about the events of Thursday afternoon. They'd talked to Rollo Kohler, heard his version of our encounter. He'd showed them the knot on his forehead and complained about his painful throat, insisting that he contemplated filing charges. He described a witness in a white SUV. I gave them my story, offering in its support my splinted hand and the fact that Rollo Kohler was much younger and rather larger than I was, and had a history of violence. I insisted that I had only defended myself, and I acknowledged that I'd spoken with the witness, who had enjoyed the fracas, but that I hadn't asked his name.

The detectives wanted to know why I had been to see Joe Kohler. I told them that I hoped he might help me learn the whereabouts of an old acquaintance of his, Howie Ragatz, who I at that time thought might have been the father of a young woman named Mia Dunn. They wanted to know why I wanted to know. I told them that I was doing Ms. Dunn a favor.

They asked questions, left me alone in the interrogation room, returned and asked the same questions again, left, returned. Finally, they told me they might want to speak to me again, and they showed me out.

I drove home, punched up Argenta playing Mendelssohn, poured Glenlivet over ice, sat in my chair, and sipped scotch. The musicians played the pieces beautifully, but I couldn't really enjoy the performance. My hand pained me, faintly, and my liver was still sore, and I was beat, not so much weary as weak. And I was disturbed.

Joe Kohler had been murdered. I hadn't been involved in a murder case in decades, but I was involved in this one, although I didn't know how or why. But even before the arthritic old thug was killed, I'd been regressing, doing what I didn't do anymore. I'd taunted Len Maglie. I'd broken into Mia Dunn's apartment. I'd been stupid and violent with Rollo Kohler. And now I'd danced the prevaricator's polka with the police.

Something had knocked me off balance. Was it Alicia's presence? My guilt? Was it Frank and his failing health and his failing will? Or was it my sense that the town and the world had irrevocably altered, that now I had no real function in either, and that I was just an old man not quite ready to confront my inevitable end?

I was retired, lived a life quiet but certainly not empty. I was single but not alone. I had Cynthia and her family, whom I visited twice a year and kept in touch with through emails and Facebook. I had Frank, our long friendship, our cribbage contests and our talks and our silences. I had acquaintances, some from high school and college, some from years dealing at the edges of the legal and law enforcement communities, some from the golf course or the gym. I went to ball games and concerts and plays. I enjoyed the desert. I read books and listened to music. I kept my home clean and tidy, and myself. I ran and worked out, had no health problems. I had no money problems. I had no problems at all.

So why was I listening to old urgings, wandering in the world I'd managed to escape years before? Was it simply that I was bored?

I thought about checking on Frank, but it was too late, he was probably asleep. An opportunity missed. These would be fewer and fewer.

Darkness settled outside my window. I turned off the music, rinsed out my glass, and put it in the dishwasher. I went to bed. Listening to the wind rattle the lid of the garbage can at the back of the house, I had a thought. The murder of Joe Kohler of course changed everything. But his was not the first death. There had been another.

SUNDAY. THE WIND blew. Snow fell in the Sierra. Rain soaked the foothills, muddied the trails, wetted the city streets. Frank was at his son's for football and dinner. I watched the 49ers' game. I read more of *The Troubled Man.* I listened to Willie and Waylon, then to Emanuel Ax playing Brahms. And I thought about things.

Most of what I'd learned so far left me with questions. About Bryce Ragatz and Harvey Prior: had the war hero been flying in dope for the sleaze merchant? That's what Len Maglie had seemed to say. He also said that Howie Ragatz had been delivering cash for him. I doubted that, but if so, from whom to whom? He dismissed the notion that the robbery of

Bryce Ragatz was important, had more or less told me to leave it alone; why then did slick Snooks want to know about it? Had Randy Barnes been doing with Bryce Ragatz's money what I suspected? If so, why? What did the photo of Randy in the hot tub with Gale Dunn actually mean, if anything? Why were Randy and Howie Ragatz enemies? Who killed Joe Kohler? Maglie or one of his thugs, Snooks, Paulie? Why?

I was in the middle of something that had started long before Mia Dunn sent a letter to Alicia Barnes. It seemed to have started when Gale Dunn began making drunken phone calls. And then she died.

TEN

Gray Monday.

The next morning, the rain reduced mostly to mist, after a run along the river I drove to the nearest Office Depot and copied the Ragatz file. Returned home, I carefully blacked out on the copy every name it contained. Then I took the redacted file to the best accountant I knew. She told me to come back in a few hours.

Frank had the cribbage board set up. He looked bad, said he thought he was getting the flu, but insisted that we play cards. As we did, I told him about my set-to with Rollo Kohler. Frank cocked an admonishing eyebrow. Then I told him about Joe Kohler.

His expression changed. "You think it's connected to this other thing?"

"If it isn't," I said, "it's a hell of a coincidence."

We played. Then I said, "I wouldn't mind seeing the autopsy report. Or at least getting the exact cause of death."

"What's in it for me?"

"My undying gratitude."

He twirled a finger in mock celebration. "Whoopee!"

He would get me what he could. He didn't ask why I wanted the information. I wasn't sure that I could actually have told him.

I did give him the details of Maglie's visit, of his suggestion that Bryce Ragatz had flown in dope for Harvey Prior. "I'd never have guessed that," Frank said.

I didn't show him the photo of Randy Barnes in the hot tub with Gale Dunn. That picture and the one taken in the Blue Flame were locked in my desk drawer with my important papers and my grandfather's .38 Smith and Wesson.

I didn't mention the Ragatz file.

Frank played listlessly, as if merely going through the motions. He looked thinner, the bones of his face jutting up under his skin. His gaze sometimes emptied, as if he were looking upon Nothing. His voice again sounded hollow. But he shrugged off my concern.

We finished our game and chat and silence, and I left him with a slightly soggy Paltry.

I drove home and called Alicia, left a message on her machine suggesting that she stop in to see her brother. Then I had lunch, took a nap. Then I went to see my accountant friend. She was in a meeting, but she'd left the file with her secretary. She'd attached to the folder a hand-written note. "Whoever did this was really good. Hiding assets in a divorce case, maybe? I'd need more time to be absolutely sure, but it looks like he disappeared about $120,000. My bill won't be quite that much."

One hundred twenty thousand dollars was enough to provide four-hundred-a-month child support for eighteen years, pay for an education at UNR, and have a down payment on a tiny blue car left over.

I called the number Carlotta Farragut Ragatz had given me. Her husband was not available. However, she wished to speak to me. In an hour. At her home.

I said I'd be there.

Had they all not fallen, leaves would still have trembled in the neighborhood celebrated by Walter Van Tilburg Clark. Now, bare wet branches arched over old narrow streets and stately homes. One of these was a handsome structure of brick and plaster built nearly a hundred years before. It dominated the neighborhood by style rather than size, spoke, in subdued tones, of substance and security, of money—not Denny Farragut's wads of sweat-dampened bills and stacks of chips but Carl Ragatz's crisp debentures and bearer bonds.

I parked at the curb and made my way up the short walk. The front door had no bell button, only a wrought-iron knocker that I gave a good whack.

Carlotta Farragut Ragatz opened the door almost immediately, which surprised me. Her taut smile surprised me as well. She had decided to be nice, apparently, or at least polite.

"Right on time, Mr. Ross. I appreciate punctuality. Rare these days."

She was in business blue, pinstriped skirt and jacket and a cerulean blouse, as if prepared to talk proposals and contracts. I'd taken the time to change into a charcoal suit and gray tie that asserted respectability. We were both in uniform.

She invited me into a small, old-fashioned atrium, complete with a gilt-edged mirror and an ancient coat tree. Beyond us, to the right, was a comfortably furnished living room, to the left a short hallway down which she led me to an open library: bright-jacketed books, writing table, a brace of wing-backed chairs. A wide window looked onto a lawn interrupted by beds of well-cared-for rose bushes. A solitary quail scurried across the wet grass.

She showed me to a seat. She again smiled her stiff-mouthed smile, even as she sat back into her chair. She would be friendly but firm, maintain the distance between us.

"I've made inquiries, Mr. Ross. You haven't been involved in anything unpleasant for many years. People say you're honest and discreet." She nodded, as if placing a period at the end of her remark. "And I'm assured by my husband that you have no agenda, mercenary or otherwise. He says you're one of us."

One of us. A native of the City of Trembling Leaves, she meant, a distinction now mere nostalgia for a time when everyone knew everyone else and social and economic inequalities were held to be of no consequence, even though they always were.

"I'd like to speak to him again," I said. "When might that be possible?"

"Not for some time," she said. The muscles at her mouth moved so stiffly she seemed a ventriloquist's dummy. "Is it something I can help you with? Has it to do with Howie Ragatz?"

"No," I said. "You might want to know that DNA says he's not Mia Dunn's father."

Out on the lawn, the quail reappeared, stopped, looked about, and stuttered off again.

"And you're no longer looking for him." She nodded, satisfied, as if she'd accomplished a strenuous task. "Good. I was going to tell you to give it up. I've decided that it was a pointless pursuit. He must be dead. How he died is of no importance."

Carlotta Farragut Ragatz had decided more than that. She'd decided, she said, that she would approach Newton Ragatz. Howie's widow was psychologically unsound and impossible to deal with, but the young man would surely be receptive to her advances. And he was, after all, her husband's only living relative, carried with him the genes to continue the Ragatz line.

The Ragatz line. I didn't tell her, because she would not have heard, that there had never been a Ragatz line. There had been Carl Ragatz and his son. Now, other than those of our dying generation, few people in the

Truckee Meadows had any idea who either were or what each had done. There had been a Ragatz moment, now passed.

"I understand that he's a wounded veteran," she said. "My husband feels strongly that that in itself is enough to earn our interest. We would like to help him, if we can. He's family."

Newton Ragatz being invited into the family from which his father had been barred. I smiled at the irony.

What, she wanted to know, could I tell her about the young man? I offered my opinion. Satisfied, she asked me to arrange for her to meet him, sometime later in the week. She thought Emile's would do nicely. She would pay me for my time.

"You might explain to him that no promises will be made."

I told her that I would be happy to set up such a meeting. "No charge."

She shifted in her seat, as if preparing to rise. She was finished. I was dismissed.

The quail was back, now running in a tight, apparently purposeless circle on the lawn.

"I still need to talk to your husband," I said.

"Again, Mr. Ross, he's unavailable." She leaned forward. "What's this about? You don't think he can tell you who sired this young woman."

"As I said the other day, he knows many of the people involved. He might be able to help, give me a lead." I watched her. She was displeased. "Then there's another matter that's come up. It has to do with some work Randy Barnes did for your husband."

She pressed back in her chair, as if to increase the distance between us. "Randy Barnes saved Bryce some money in taxes. That was many years ago."

"It's probably nothing," I said. "Alicia was emptying out a safe Randy used at home and came across a file. It documents some unusual financial dealings."

Her face darkened. "And you are accusing my husband of what, exactly?"

"Nothing, Mrs. Ragatz." I gave her my most ingenuous smile. "No accusations. Just a couple of questions."

Then she offered her own smile, the cruel one. "Alicia—your ex-wife—she has aspirations. Boards, committees. I can make sure these are never achieved."

It was time I backed out of this. "Mrs. Ragatz, I have no intention of causing trouble for you or your husband. And you and I both know that Alicia would never do anything to injure or offend you."

Her color deepened. "You seem not to know your ex-wife as well as you think you do, Mr. Ross."

When she didn't explain, I said, "The questions I have, Mrs. Ragatz, are not about your husband. They're about Alicia's husband. I can't say any more until I talk to Bryce, not even to you, I'm afraid."

She studied me, debating. Then she rose. "Bryce is attending to some business up at the lake that should take him through the evening. He'll be at the cabin after nine or so tonight."

On the lawn there suddenly appeared a covey of quail, adult and young. They skittered, stopped, looked about as if waiting for something to happen. Then in an explosion of gray they were gone.

She gave me directions to their cabin. I thanked her. I told her that I'd get back to her about meeting with Newton Ragatz. She showed me out.

For a moment I stood on the sidewalk, wondering what Alicia could have done to earn the animus of Carlotta Farragut Ragatz.

A faint drizzle grayed the desert as I pulled up onto Merle Stafford's lot. I realized then that I should have called. The place looked, felt deserted. The shop door was shut and padlocked, the carport empty. The remains of the barn were gone, leaving a blackened rectangle of muddied ash, the faint tang of fire.

To be sure that no one was about, I parked by the house and climbed to the porch. My knock echoed emptily. I was about to leave when the door inched open. Laurel Stafford looked out at me, as if from hiding.

"Good afternoon, Mrs. Stafford," I said. "I was looking for your son."

She didn't remember me. I smiled. "I'm Jack Ross. I was here the other day. I need to speak to Newt."

"Oh," she said. She smiled, as if fulfilling a duty. "Please come in, won't you?"

I stepped into a room furnished with good wood and brightly patterned cloth. A vase held artificial flowers, a bowl waxed fruit. Walls were papered in subdued stripes and adorned with framed photographs of idyllic landscapes. On the thick-napped beige carpet, clear plastic runners made trails to couch and chairs and on through an archway to a dining room and more highly polished wood: table, sideboard, and armoire. Neither room showed any sign of having been lived in.

"Please be seated," she said. "May I offer you something?"

I declined. She perched at the edge of the couch, legs crossed primly at the ankles, hands clasped in her lap. Her linen dress spread out stiffly. She looked at me, seemed bewildered, at a loss about what to do or say.

"You have a nice home," I said simply to break the silence.

She nodded. "I wanted it when I was a little girl."

I didn't know what that meant. I tried again. "I was hoping to see your husband. Will he be back soon?"

"Oh no," she said. "He's dead."

Now I was bewildered. I gave it one more go. "I also need to talk to your son. You must be glad to have him back?"

"Back?" She looked around the room, as if for something she'd misplaced, then repeated herself. "Back?"

I felt, sitting with this strange, beautiful woman, a deepening sorrow. And shame. I felt that I was a voyeur, violating her special privacy.

I got abruptly to my feet. "I'm afraid I don't have time to wait. Mrs. Stafford. But I do need to talk with Newt. Could you ask him to give me a call?"

She didn't answer but rose too and followed me to the door. As I stepped out onto the porch, Merle Stafford drove the Audi into the lot. Seeing me with his wife, he slammed the car to a halt and jerked open the door and advanced swiftly. We met at the foot of the stairs.

"What are you doing here?" His face was flushed. His eyes were hard. His hands were fists. "What do you want?"

"At ease, Gunny," I said quietly.

He leaned forward, tense, quivering. I'd seen that before, trembling men eager to attack. "Fucking lawyers. I should have known."

I looked at him steadily. Finally, he took a deep breath, slowly releasing it, along with some of the tension in his body. "Yeah. Okay. I don't know what she told you, but she's not . . . she's not . . ." He couldn't get it out. "You didn't ask her about Howie?"

"No."

He was still angry. He was afraid that she might have told me something.

With a painful-sounding scrape, he cleared his throat. "What were you talking about?"

"I've been here about two minutes, Gunny," I said. "I need to talk to Newt, but not about his father. I'm not looking for Howie Ragatz and don't much care what happened to him. I didn't ask your wife about anything."

I told him that Carlotta Farragut Ragatz wanted to meet Newt. I told him why. "Have him call me, will you?"

After a moment he sighed. His fists unfolded. "It's just . . ."

"I know. You take care of her."

"No, you don't know. Not really."

"I know it's none of my business," I said.

"Yeah." He stilled. "I get a little touchy, I guess."

He walked me to my car, but before I could open the door, he said, "Look, Ross—there's coffee in the shop. And maybe Newt will show up. He's doing an installation, could be back any time."

He didn't want coffee. But he wanted something. We went over to the shop.

The interior was neat, tidy, redolent of sawdust and machine oil and, soon, brewing coffee. I looked over his saws and drills and planes and routing tables and sanders, gluing vices and staining racks, and I admired the efficiency of their arrangement. He handed me a cup of coffee, motioned me to a stool at a drafting table, and pulled up another.

"There's a lot we don't know," he said.

About his wife, he meant. He had pieces, bits, some of which he got from her, some from her sister Bonnie, who had made brief contact with them ten years earlier, some from an agency he'd hired to look into her history. What he knew was grim. She had been failed.

Her mother was alcoholic, her father lame and addicted to schemes and petty crime. With their three daughters, Heck and Louisa Downs left Minot, North Dakota, to drift around the West, living in shacks and seedy motels and, for periods, their old rattle-trap Ford, on the run from debts and threats, from the law, from welfare and truant officers. They conned charities and suckered social services, pilfered and scammed and begged. As Laurel and her two older sisters grew, their parents came more and more to rely on them to steal, scam, and sell whatever they had that someone might buy. In Boise, Idaho, Laurel's sister, Kate, fifteen, was arrested for solicitation. Shortly thereafter, in Santa Fe, Louisa Downs died. Six months later, in Rock Springs, Wyoming, Kate climbed into the cab of a long-distance hauler and rode off without a wave goodbye. Heck Downs raged, and his two remaining daughters suffered until Laurel's other sister, Bonnie, finally turned to child protective agents. For five years then, from the time she was nine, Laurel lived in a series of foster homes, in at least one of which she was sexually abused. Until, at fourteen, she appeared on the streets of Bakersfield. She roamed with a loose pack of drug-addled teenagers who survived by breaking into homes, stealing from stores, mugging elderly men and women, and selling their blood and their bodies. Arrested a few times, charges dropped. Fresno, Sacramento, Tahoe. Until at eighteen, alone, now in Reno, she found work waiting tables in the coffee shop of the Claim Jumper Casino.

Compounding, intensifying all this was her beauty. She was a beautiful child, a beautiful girl, and beautiful young woman. She was also, early on, odd.

In Reno, she attracted gazes. As she always had. Which she ignored. She had learned long before to disconnect, to escape people behind an empty smile. Others made of her what they would. Some found her mysterious, bewitching, and enticing. Some suspected a mental deficiency, others sexual and emotional repression. But now she served diners and smiled her empty smile and ignored the eyes and declined the invitations and remained unattached. She roomed with another waitress in a small apartment on Stardust Street. She spent her off hours sleeping or paging through magazines like *House Beautiful*. On her twenty-first birthday, she began serving drinks to good-tipping gamblers who hoped they might get lucky. They didn't, at least not with Laurel Downs. No one did.

Then she married Howie Ragatz. She married him, Merle Stafford said, because he promised to build her a house. Why he married her was, to all who knew him, a conundrum. Merle Stafford could only surmise.

"She—people see her, see how beautiful she is, and the way she is, and they try to fit her into their fantasies."

I wasn't sure I understood that, but I didn't say so. "And Howie Ragatz?"

"Stupid stuff." Stafford looked into his coffee cup. "He thought he could make her a sort of prize, that she could get him into the Ragatz family circle. Stupid bastard."

His gaze, his expression, his voice all softened. I saw again what I'd seen the day we met. He was tired. He was a burdened man struggling to stand upright.

"And now, Gunny?"

"Yeah," he said. He coughed. "I know. After Howie disappeared, even before, maybe, she started to . . . drift off. Shrinks call it clinical depression, because they have to call it something, but they don't really know. But she takes her meds, she's not unhappy, even if she doesn't quite really feel." He fell silent. Then he looked at me. "She doesn't leave the house much. She takes care of it. And we take care of her, Newt and me."

"You seem to be doing a good job of it."

"So far. Maybe. But the Corps didn't train us for this sort of thing."

"Sure it did," I said. "Semper Fi."

I stood up. "I don't want to upset her. But something's going on, Gunny, and people aren't telling me everything they know."

He rose too. "Like you said, some things are just none of your business."

"Maybe," I said. "But things are happening, and they seem to be connected. Like your barn being torched."

I'd thought to jar him into revelation. He didn't blink.

"Joe Kohler is dead."

He nearly smiled. “Good.”

I waited, but he didn’t ask the obvious questions. Maybe because he already knew the answers. Or maybe just because he didn’t care.

“You knew Gale Dunn?”

“Who she was,” he said. “I seen her dance a couple of times. She breathed sex.”

“She’s dead too.” I moved to the door. “That’s two. You need to be careful, Gunny, you and Newt. We don’t want it to be three.”

ELEVEN

The Douglas County courthouse sat serenely in the gloomy wet late afternoon, solid gray stone with a wide stairway leading to a gracefully pillared porch. The architecture argued that within, reason ruled and justice prevailed. I was in favor of both, but all I'd driven down to Minden for was a little information.

Soon I had it. A couple of conversations and a look at the sheriff's report and the record of the autopsy confirmed what Mia Dunn had told me about her mother's death. Photographs showed her neck angled askew. The pathologist affirmed that she had suffered a "hangman's fracture," a broken C2 vertebra. She died, her blood alcohol reading said, blotto.

I'd looked carefully at the photos. The auburn hair that once fell to her shoulders was cropped short and shot with gray. The face was that of a middle-aged woman who'd spent too much time in the desert sun. The body that had once urged advances from males of the species was a lumpy mass in an old sweatshirt and worn jeans.

I looked at the photographs, and for a moment all that I'd been doing for the past week became unreal, the way that war sometimes suddenly felt like a daydream, a fantasy. Then they became just photographs of a dead woman again.

I'd learned nothing of obvious interest. I didn't know why I'd thought I might. Nor did I know why Gale Dunn's death troubled me. But I was beginning to sense a shape to things—old desires and money and murder.

Headed back north, on impulse I turned off at the road leading to the Dunn place. The alfalfa fields were dark with damp. The place looked deserted, even forlorn under the ragged gray sky. The screen on the front door of the house hung open and aslant.

I parked and got out and looked over the equipment in the shed. Implements lined up in a neat row—cutting blades, rakes, balers, some stand-alone, others attachments for the tractor. The green, long-snouted John Deere diesel was almost as old as I was, as beat up and bent in places.

I tried to envision what had happened. Severely inebriated, Gale Dunn had been in the tractor seat, started to climb down, missed her step, and fell, banging her head against the hard rubber of a rear tire before she hit the ground head first with force enough to snap her neck. The sheriff's detectives had reconstructed the events that way, and I had no reason to question the scenario.

She died on a Friday night. The body lay out of sight from the road and wasn't found until Monday, when a mail carrier arrived to deliver a handful of political flyers and a utility bill. Scavengers had been at her, crows, coyotes. Nothing at the scene suggested that the death of Gale Dunn was not an alcohol-induced mishap.

The only question that remained unanswered was what in the hell she was doing sitting on a tractor in the dark. No one knew.

I thought about checking out the house, but I had no idea what to look for. I doubted that I could find anything that Mia Dunn might have passed over. I wondered then about the young woman. How was she doing, and what? She'd started all this and now seemed almost irrelevant to it.

I got back in my car and pulled away.

Bryce Ragatz wouldn't be at his cabin for a good while yet, so in the waning of the day I drove back to Reno, to Frank's house, where the sight of Alicia's BMW in the driveway deterred me from stopping. I couldn't talk to Frank about what I'd learned while his sister was there. I kept going, headed home, ate a sandwich, and watched the news—chaos, corruption, crime. Then I went out into darkness.

Mist turned to fog, fog to clouds that spit snow as I turned off the freeway onto the Mount Rose Highway and started up the Sierra. The old road followed the foothills' gradual grade through sage and rabbit brush, as dark strips of tarmac led off to the lights of newer homes clustered at the base of the mountains. Pine thickened as the slope steepened and the highway narrowed through gulches and edged past drop-offs, and more new roads headed toward more homes and gated communities partially visible through the trees.

Snow began to stick on pine branches and hillsides, to swirl and stutter in my headlights. Not far beyond the Montreux Country Club, a recently repaved and unmarked road swung into the trees. I took it, and in a quarter mile or so I came to a gate, which stood open, and a panel of buttons and screens that seemed a system defunct. Snow flurried as I advanced.

Marcellus Ridge was a collection of patented properties—meadow, pasture, seep, and spring—amid Forest Service lands that the developer had somehow gained title to. Now multimillion-dollar homes, most arranged at the edges of the well-thinned timberland, looked out over rills and ponds and swales and stands of aspen and, far off through the storm, the glow of the evening lights of Reno and Sparks. It was Caughlin Ranch hundreds of feet higher and millions of dollars dearer. What Carlotta Farragut Ragatz had called a cabin was a three-layered sprawl across the base of a rocky ledge. Lights gleamed in the large window beside the front door.

I parked in a patch of carefully graded and raked gravel. In the open garage sat the Mercedes convertible I'd seen at the Stead airport. Two files in hand, I went to the front door, pressed the bell, and, as I waited, let the snow settle cold and wet on my upturned face.

Bryce Ragatz answered the door, flushed, damp with sweat that stained his UNR workout togs and headband. "Lottie said you'd be up, Jack." His smile became a grin. "I hope this won't take long. I'm expecting a guest."

I stepped inside. The large, high-ceilinged room suggested the rustic: rug-strewn hardwood floor, mahogany and leather furniture, a large rock fireplace in which paper and kindling and logs awaited fire. Watercolors gave the walls skiing and fishing scenes. On the mantle rested photographs, informal shots of youthful and middle-aged Bryce and Carlotta together, as well as a photo of a smiling Carlotta chatting with Ronald Reagan and one of Bryce in his Reno High basketball uniform. Doors led, I assumed, to other levels and rooms.

Ragatz waved me to a large couch. Sitting, I handed him the copied and redacted file. "Randy Barnes's widow found this."

He took the folder to the other end of the couch. "What am I looking at here, Ross?"

I told him what my accountant friend had told me. After giving him a moment to take it in, I said, "The obvious question is why you would have Randy Barnes squeeze over a hundred thousand dollars from your various accounts."

"That slick son-of-a-bitch," he said quietly. He wasn't angry. He was amused. "The answer to that obvious question is, I didn't."

"Then Randy stole your money," I said. "That doesn't trouble you?"

"Surprises me." His shrug was slight, as if he could hardly be bothered to react. "I wouldn't have thought he was the type. But it was a long time ago. And he saved me a lot more than that, over the years, in taxes. Besides, what can I do about it? He's dead."

Bryce Ragatz's cool was founded on supreme confidence. Nothing could come that he couldn't handle. Maybe that was why he flew warplanes that made excellent targets and took over casinos that were losing money and pursued the wives of other men. In any case, now he was pretty clearly telling the truth.

He smiled again. "I'm guessing Alicia didn't know about this. What did he need the money for? He have a dolly on the side?"

I handed him the other file, let him glance over the letters from the bank to Gale Dunn and her daughter before I said, "Looks like he used the money to provide for Mia Dunn and her education. Why would he have done that?"

"I suppose," he said, "because he thought he was her father and wanted to help her."

"But why take the money from you?"

Ragatz got up and went to a sideboard on which stood a row of bottles. He held up a fifth of Grey Goose. "Care to?"

I declined. I still had a drive through darkness and snow down a steep and winding road.

He hadn't answered my question. "Since we're supposing, suppose Randy didn't think he was Mia's father. Suppose he thought you were, thought you should support her."

He pondered it as he poured himself a drink. "Could be."

"Did he have good reason to suppose that?"

He tasted his drink. "Who knows? People talk."

That wasn't really an answer. "I know you preferred married women—the danger, the intrigue, all that—but you had a yen for Gale Dunn. And she belonged to Harvey Prior, which would add some hazard to the effort."

He took his drink to the fireplace, leaned lazily against the mantle, and looked at, seemed to speak to the image of his young athletic self. "Lots of men slept with Gale. Anyway, what difference does it make now?"

"A lot, to Mia Dunn at least," I said. "On the other hand, it doesn't make any difference at all to you. Why don't you just do a DNA test and we'll know for sure."

"No." He leaned back, wholly at ease. "If it happened that my sperm did the deed, Ross, word would inevitably get out. I wouldn't want that." His smile slipped away. "Our marriage, Carlotta's and mine, is really an alliance, a set of agreements. One of them is that neither of us will do anything to embarrass the other."

Not love but loyalty. "But you can hardly be concerned with your reputation. You're a dedicated philanderer, and everybody who knows you knows it."

"And no one cares. Certainly not Lottie. She knows about all my . . . adventures. She could give you a list. And she has her own way of handling the women I've frolicked with."

I wasn't sure what that meant, but I didn't worry about it. "I still don't see the problem."

"It's a personal matter," he said quietly, with a seriousness he hadn't demonstrated before. "We are childless. Nothing wrong with either of us, the doctors say, it just never happened. That's always been an issue for her, makes her feel inadequate, gives small-minded people reason to speculate about all kinds of things, our sex life among them. The idea that I might have a child with another woman would give her grief."

It wasn't an especially compelling reason, but I let it go. Lots of people did and felt lots of things for reasons that weren't especially compelling.

I shifted gears. "So why does she want me to stop looking for Howie?"

Now he laughed, a lazy chuckle. "Because she thinks you'll find out that I killed him."

He seemed to enjoy my reaction. He returned to the couch, sat, slipped out of his headband and ran his hand through his damp greying hair.

"It was Gale, her drunken phone call to Carlotta. She accused me of killing Howie. She had all kinds of reasons. Jealousy of his success with her. Anger at his smearing the Ragatz name. Other stuff."

"Did you? Kill him, I mean?"

He smiled. The silence stretched. It didn't perturb him.

I was going to have to work my way through it. "Did the other stuff include the fact that Howie was in on the robbery that cost Paulie Hauberk his hand?"

His smile didn't flicker. "Get far enough away from something, sometimes it's a lot easier to see it clearly, huh?"

"The robbery that netted the robbers nothing."

His smile brightened.

It was my turn to laugh. "Let me tell you what I think, Bryce. The two men with Dick Pym were Joe Kohler and Howie. Kohler shot Paulie Hauberk, and Howie ended up with your attaché case. It had enough money in it to give the three a healthy split, money you got from Harvey Prior for drugs you flew into the country for him."

"Drugs?" He feigned mild alarm. "My goodness! That would be against the law."

"But a lot of fun," I said. "You'd have enjoyed doing business with thugs, outwitting the law, flying by the seat of your pants, risking your reputation and your business and your life."

"Think what you want, Ross," he said easily. "You can't prove any of it."

I shrugged. "Why would I want to prove it? The statute of limitations on the drug stuff is long past." I changed directions again. "How did you know it was Howie?"

He laughed again. "The nitwit. I knew him right away, his shape, his posture, his voice."

"Did you know the third guy was Joe Kohler too?"

He shook his head. "I never much cared who it was. I don't know a Joe Kohler."

"So you didn't beat him to death with a tire iron the other day."

Finally, something surprised him. "Beat him to de—what the hell's going on, Ross?"

"I don't know," I said. "Another thing I don't know is why Len Maglie insists that the money Howie had belonged to him."

"He claims it's his?" he said. He paused thoughtfully. "I'd never heard that."

Lights flared briefly in the dark square that was the window.

He drained his drink. "What has all this to do with who fathered Gale's child?"

"Not much," I said, "Not in itself. It's just that when I ask about that, I keep running into this other crap. Somehow it all centers on Cousin Howie."

Outside, tires crunched gravel. Bryce Ragatz smiled. "Time for you to go, Ross."

"Sure," I said. "I wouldn't want to interfere with an adventure. If that's what you're still up to."

As the doorbell rang, he grinned. "We're the luckiest generation of males in the history of the human race, Jack. At the very moment we needed it, along came Viagra."

The snow had stopped. The fog had thinned. Far off in the darkness, Reno and Sparks sat in a lambent bowl.

I drove back to the highway and started down the mountain. Traffic was sparse, the road wet. Snow whitened the forest. For a mile or so I followed red taillights that brightened at curves until, finally, they turned into the trees and disappeared. An approaching truck momentarily lit up the night with its high beams. Then darkness again.

As I attended to the twists and curls of the road, watching my headlights butt against rocky outcrops or hang in the darkness over sharp declines, I tried to assess what I'd learned from Bryce Ragatz. He'd confirmed my guesses about the robbery—except, I realized, I still didn't know why he would be taking money into his casino. Or how Howie Ragatz would know his cousin was carrying an attaché case full of cash.

Bryce Ragatz might very well have been the father of Mia Dunn. I could soon be sure, one way or the other: I had his sweat-stained headband stuffed into my jacket pocket.

And I'd more or less determined that Ragatz had been hauling drugs for Harvey Prior.

But none of this spoke to the only real question I wanted answered—had Randy Barnes been faithful to his wife?

Bryce and Carlotta Farragut Ragatz had a relationship based on loyalty, not love.

Randy Barnes had loved Alicia, but had he been loyal? Or had he been, just a bit, bored? Had he, trying to help a sexually attractive woman, allowed himself to be overwhelmed by her? Seduced? Suckered? I still didn't know.

I drove out of the snow as I descended. Then headlights snapped on at a turn-off thirty yards ahead. When I passed, a light-colored old sedan pulled onto the highway behind me. High beams lit up my mirror, got brighter fast. Too fast. I eased over onto the narrow shoulder at the edge of a drop, but the sedan accelerated and thumped my rear bumper, hard, and thumped again, harder, and a front wheel dipped, the rear end slued, and suddenly I was over the edge, braking desperately, pointlessly, sliding down as tree trunks flashed by until, in a sudden flip and roll, my head banged against the window and I heard the screeching scrape of a skid that ended with a jolt as the front end hit a tree.

I was all right.

I was okay.

I was fine.

The Subaru was on its right side. I was harnessed securely in my seatbelt. Only the passenger airbag had deployed. I'd banged my head and chest and knee, but I was fine.

The dead engine ticked in the sudden huge silence. The headlights carved a yellow shaft into the darkness. I was okay. I was all right.

I smelled gasoline. I had to get out.

My seatbelt unbuckled easily. My door was jammed shut. The power windows worked only when the engine was running. I smelled gasoline.

With my good, left hand I banged on the window, but to no effect. I smelled gasoline. I feared fire.

I hit the window again, harder. Nothing. Raising up off the seat, I struck out as hard as I could with my elbow but felt only a slight give. I couldn't generate force enough. I was trapped, I was going to die, I was going to burn to death because I was too old and fucking feeble to break a pane of automobile glass.

Mindlessly, I hammered my elbow into the window. Then it exploded. A sledge-like black slab busted away chunks of shattered glass. A hand reached in and grabbed me by the shirt front and pulled.

I got the idea. Soon I had my head and shoulders out of the car. Bits of window scraped at my groin and thighs and shins as I squirmed and shimmied and fell out finally at the feet of Paulie Hauberk.

Without a word, he turned and started back up to the highway. I tried to follow his square shadow, but the incline was slick with wet pine needles, and I was wobbly, and I hurt. My chest heaved painfully, my lungs burned. My head and knee ached. Twenty yards from the edge of the embankment, I had to stop.

Up on the roadway, a glare of lights swelled, engines sounded, voices. Human shadows appeared and started down the slope. Flashlights beamed. When men reached me, I was alone.

A Washoe County Sheriff's Department cruiser showed up as passers-by helped me up to the highway. Paulie Hauberk was nowhere in sight. Then EMTs arrived, and although I didn't think I needed treatment, I didn't argue when they stuck me in their van and hooked me up to their machines. At the Renown South Meadows Emergency Room, staff doctors charted my bruises and abrasions but determined that I was not seriously injured. Staff nurses made me comfortable. One of the nurses was Mia Dunn. Her smile was small and wan.

Through all this I provided medical information, signed insurance forms, and expressed relief that I was relatively uninjured and that there had been no fire after all.

Finally, officers of the law and doctors in authority agreed that I could leave. Tomorrow there would be more forms, and a written statement for the sheriff.

I took a taxi home. I stood in the shower for a long time. Then I limped into bed, but for a long while I didn't sleep.

TWELVE

I awoke near noon, sore, depressed, old. I'd suffered a bruised sternum and knee. My lungs still hurt and my broken hand ached again. And I felt deeply, profoundly inept. I'd been taken, easily. Twenty, even ten years before, I'd have avoided the smash-up, one way or another. But now my instincts were dull, my reflexes shot. I was basically useless.

I had a prescription for pain pills, but I decided not to fill it unless I absolutely had to. Maybe a little suffering would teach me to pay attention.

I had phone messages. Newt Ragatz would meet with Carlotta Farragut Ragatz. Mia Dunn hoped I was feeling better.

Her call reminded me of what I'd taken from Bryce Ragatz. I found the sweatband, slipped it into a baggie, and stuffed it in my pocket.

The storm had passed, the sky emptied, the temperature dropped. After making myself presentable, I took a taxi to the sheriff's office on Parr Boulevard, where I wrote out a full statement about the incident. I told them that I'd had only a glimpse of the sedan, which might have been tan or brown, and hadn't seen the driver.

The deputy asked who had known I would be on the Mount Rose Highway that night. I told her Bryce Ragatz and his wife. She didn't know who they were.

I was lucky, she said. I might have been killed. Maybe it was a drunk. Maybe it was kids. Maybe it was a mistake. In any case, it was attempted murder, so detectives would investigate, but the deputy doubted much would come of it.

The night before, I hadn't mentioned Paulie Hauberk. I didn't now. He had helped me, although I wasn't sure why, and I could see no reason to get him tangled up with the law.

Neither did I tell anyone about Rollo Kohler. There was no point. He'd have stolen and dumped the old sedan. He'd have an alibi.

Finished with the sheriff, I winced and limped through the afternoon. I taxied to a car rental outfit on South Virginia and took a two-year-old Lexus, which I drove to the office of my insurance agent. My policy covered the cost of the rental, and I'd soon receive a settlement check for my totaled Subaru, which had been hauled to a wrecking yard on West Fourth. I went over there and gave a grimy young man twenty dollars to help me go through the car. The Ragatz file papers were scattered over the seat and floor. I made sure I got them all. Finally, I drove to the DNA lab and left the bagged sweatband and told them what I wanted. Forty-eight hours, at least, they said.

By now it was nearly five, and I'd had enough. Too much, in fact. I felt woozy, aquiver, not quite in control of my body. I recognized the condition. Delayed shock. We'd experienced it in Nam, some of us, some of the time, a day or so after a fierce firefight.

I made it home and managed to cook and consume an omelet, which along with a glass of wine had me feeling better. I called Carlotta Farragut Ragatz, got a machine, and relayed Newton Ragatz's message and gave her his number. I called Mia Dunn, got a machine, assured her that I was doing fine and that I wanted soon to talk to her about her mother's death. Then I called Frank. He sounded weak, distant. When I told him what had happened on the Mount Rose Highway, he paused, then said, "I thought you didn't do this sort of thing anymore."

I poured myself more wine and turned on the television to catch the news. Somehow nothing had changed, but everything was worse. French authorities were still tracking terrorists who had attacked Paris. A typhoon was ravaging Japan, and a Central American country was on the verge of revolution, and the Middle East was burning, and we were creeping into a village toward the sound of AK-47s and huts caught fire and an old woman looked out through the smoke and flames melted her face and the barn wall collapsed as Merle Stafford hurled shovel loads of dirt on the small streams of fire that seeped from beneath my Subaru and twisted like runnels of lava around the gas tank and down toward the window on which I was banging, banging . . .

Ringing, ringing. My phone. I struggled out of sleep. I mumbled a hello.

Mia Dunn's little girl voice peeped at me. I asked her to repeat herself, and this time through I got it. Was I all right? Why did I want to speak to her about her mother's death? Could we meet tomorrow? At Good Beans again? Same time? I said yes to all but the second question, which I ignored. Still half sleep-drugged, I clicked off the phone.

I'd slept nearly three hours. I switched off the television and sat and almost dropped off again but caught myself, so I was alert enough to hear a car pull into my drive. Not waiting for a knock, I got up and hobbled to the door.

As if in another dream, Alicia stood at the edge of the darkness. "Are you all right, Jack?"

Sleep or surprise robbed me of my voice. Silently, I stepped aside. She hesitated, quickly recovered, and, faintly fragrant, moved past me.

"I stopped to check on Frank. He told me what happened." she said. "I thought I'd better see how you were doing. Maybe we could talk. If you're up to it."

"I'm fine, Alicia," I said. "Sit, please. Can I get you something—wine, scotch, or I can make coffee, or tea if you prefer."

I took her coat, and she settled onto the couch, collecting her hands in her lap as if to confine them. She glanced about nervously. She had never been in my home. "A little white wine would be very nice, Jack."

I limped to the sideboard and the bottle I'd opened at dinner. While I poured her a glass of Liebfraumilch, she took in the room. What she saw should have reassured her of my old-fogy normalcy: refinished hardwood floor and small area rugs and pieces of good heavy furniture, a bookcase filled with tomes on the history of the American West and the Vietnam War; in another bookcase an arrangement of sound system and CDs; a flat-screen television; on select horizontal surfaces a scatter of desert detritus—rock, wood, iron; and on walls, framed desertscapes, both photos and watercolors by local artists.

A table beside my reading chair supported family photographs. The oldest, tinted in the 1920s mode, fixed my grandparents on their wedding day. Another had the two of them, fifteen years older, standing behind the seated dark, pretty, sullen girl who would become my mother. Pictures on a plastic block followed my daughter from kindergarten to UNR graduation. A formal portrait of her and her new husband was flanked by the latest school pictures of their son and daughter. The most recent photograph, a relaxed if studied pose before a Christmas tree, included the four of them as well as, carefully distanced, Alicia and myself.

Alicia studied the photos. "I always forget how much you favor your grandfather."

I got his size, the set of his shoulders, the jaw line. I didn't think I actually looked like him. Alicia always had. She hadn't liked Chet Stander, had heeded tales about the brutality of sheriff's deputies when he worked for the county, suspected that he'd driven my mother from home, and didn't understand my loyalty to him.

I handed her a wine glass, then made my way to my chair.

Alicia frowned. "Are you sure you're all right?"

I dismissed my injuries, which, although I'd stiffened up, in fact were giving me less discomfort. Because she asked, I offered a brief account of the wreck.

She listened with bowed her head, like a penitent seeking absolution. "Is this because of me, Jack? Because of what you're doing for me?"

"Not really," I said. "Maybe that's how it started. I think I've stumbled into an old mess, one that somebody doesn't want me mucking around in."

"And this mess," she said softly, "It involves Randy? He's part of it?"

Her face was etched with anxiety. I didn't want to add to it. But I'd promised to report honestly whatever I learned.

I told her about the disappearance of Howie Ragatz, the robbery of Bryce Ragatz, and the death of Joe Kohler, assuring her that Randy Barnes had had nothing to do with any of this. Then I told her what the file she'd found seemed to mean.

She took a small sip of wine, as if for fortification. "You're saying he stole Bryce Ragatz's money to give to a . . . to a . . ."

Alicia seemed to have suffered a body blow. Her torso bent protectively, her hands trembled, her voice hollowed.

"Bryce Ragatz and I talked about this, Alicia," I said. "We think Randy must have believed that Bryce was the father of Gale Dunn's daughter."

That got her attention. "Was he? Bryce Ragatz?"

I shrugged. "He allows it's a possibility. He doesn't know it, but in a couple of days DNA will tell us one way or the other."

"And if he isn't?" Not waiting for an answer, she set her shoulders in resolve. "I want you to let it go, Jack. Now. It doesn't matter. It's not important enough to get people hurt over."

"The DNA test is in the works," I said. "Why don't we wait for the results?"

"I don't care anymore, Jack. Randy's dead. And it's only . . ." She looked at me, then quickly looked away, "adultery."

As carefully as I could, I said, "Mia Dunn cares, Alicia. And I promised her I'd help her find out who her father was."

She flushed, instantly at the edge of anger. "But a promise to—she's nothing to you, Jack, and I'm . . . I'm . . ." She looked past me, as if I might be obscuring, hiding something of value. "I'm nothing too, I guess."

"You're the wife of my youth, Alicia."

I didn't know why I said that. I didn't even know what it meant. But she seemed to, nodding as if to certify the statement.

She took up her wine glass, looked into it. "As I said, I stopped to see Frank. He's . . ." Again color crept up her throat, this time announcing not only anger but also anxiety. "He's shutting down, Jack, shutting us out, me, his children, his . . . life. I don't understand why he's just given up! Why he won't fight! It's like he feels betrayed, feels that Sheila's awful death broke some deal he'd made with God, even though he doesn't believe in God anymore."

I shared her frustration. I had nothing to contribute. We sat in silence. Then Alicia said quietly, "Once Frank's gone, the only one I'll have left is you."

I didn't know quite what to say. "Oh, you'll have Cynthia and the grandkids, your nephews and their families, friends—"

"No," she said, shaking her head slowly, "Not that. I mean, you'll be the only one who will remember the same world I do, my parents, Frank and me when we were young, the way things used to be."

I understood. I'd long known that my dead grandparents would die again with me. I nodded but said nothing.

She smiled an odd, unhappy, artificial smile. "Did you ever cheat on me when we were married, Jack?"

I didn't know quite what was going on. "No," I said.

"Not even after you left, before the decree was final, not even then?"

Not even then. I hadn't been tempted, for months. I'd wanted to believe that it was sex, the urgencies and imperatives of the body, that ultimately caused Alicia and me so much pain. I didn't sleep with a woman until long after I'd returned from Vietnam.

"No," I said.

"No," she echoed. Her mouth twisted bitterly. "You wouldn't have."

I waited, expecting an angry accusation of some sort, but it didn't come.

She settled within herself. "Carlotta Farragut Ragatz came through. We're getting calls, promises."

I didn't tell her that Carlotta Ragatz also wanted me to stop what I was doing. I didn't ask her what she had done long ago to anger Bryce Ragatz's wife. I just smiled and told her that I was glad I'd been able to help.

She sipped her wine. She started to speak, then didn't.

I'd told her everything I knew for sure. The rest of what I had was guess, surmise, and rumor, which I wouldn't mention unless it was confirmed. I didn't show her the photograph of her husband in a hot tub with a topless dancer. I didn't know what it meant. Or so I told myself.

She stared pensively into her wine glass. At last, as if shrugging out of a constricting garment, she looked up, glanced around the room. “This is all very masculine, Jack. A man-cave, a den for an old he-bear.”

I smiled. “It suits me.”

Her smile brightened, went unreal again. “You never remarried.”

“No.” I could see that she wanted me to say more. “Came close a couple of times, but things just didn’t work out.”

“I—was it us?” Her smile now was a glare she could hide behind. “Was it me?”

We hadn’t been married a month before I knew that I’d made a mistake. For a while I thought I could live with it, and I tried to. Finally, I ran. I ran for my life.

“No,” I said again. “I don’t do intimacy well. I do best alone.”

She seemed to accept that. “Frank told me once that you married me because you wanted to be part of a family, our family.”

“I’ve heard him on that theory,” I said.

“And even though we split, you stayed part of the family. At least for Frank. For Randy too, for that matter. That used to really upset me.” It seemed it might upset her even now. “I got rid of you, but you wouldn’t go away. I mean, my parents didn’t want to ever set eyes on you again, but my brother, my husband, they were still your friends.”

“It was a long time ago, Alicia.”

She took a swallow of wine. “It won’t be that long before it will be fifty years since our wedding.”

“Time flies when you’re having fun,” I said.

She flushed again, angrily. She stood. “That’s it, Jack. Joke.”

“Sorry. Habit.”

I got up and helped her into her coat, followed her to the door. Alicia didn’t respond when I said good night. I watched her climb into her car, back out, and drive off.

I went back to my chair, but I couldn’t get comfortable. It all seemed odd now, Alicia’s smiles and glares, her skipping from topic to topic, but not quite, I sensed, randomly. She had wanted to say something but never got it out. What that might have been I didn’t know.

My earlier nap had taken the edge off my fatigue. I was still tired and sore, but at the same time I was antsy, unsettled. Bored. Frustrated. I felt an old, familiar urge. It was time to do something.

But I didn’t move. I found myself staring at the photographs. My grandfather in particular seemed to stare back at me.

Chet Stander had been the most important man in my life. I loved and, growing up, tried to be like him. Some people in Reno faulted me for this. My grandfather had been a deputy sheriff in an era when too many Nevada peace officers were little better than thugs: hijackers and burglars and thieves, extortionists and pimps, strong-arm specialists. He was not one of these, but neither was he an informer. Caught in a conflict of loyalties, he chose to say nothing about what he had seen done by men who wore a badge. His silence allowed people to assume that he too was venal and violent. He retired as soon as he could, got a P.I. license, and went to work for and then bought out a small-time bail bondsman.

He labored in a world of petty crime and small outrages, and the more respectable among the citizenry assumed that he was corrupt. He wasn't. He was, by his own lights, an honorable man. He kept his word. He tried, not always successfully, to be fair. His values were those of the heroes of American popular culture, but for all that, admirable, at least to me—courage, loyalty, honesty, and steadfastness.

Not that he was faultless. He could judge hastily and harshly, be rude, stubborn. He often oversimplified situations and motives. He didn't easily forgive, and he never forgot. But he didn't lie, he didn't cheat, he didn't steal. He was big and tough and sometimes resorted to physical force, but no more than he deemed necessary. He was a man for whom personal integrity was so central to his sense of himself that he never thought about it.

Growing up, I tried to be like him. Then I betrayed everything I thought I stood for, and as a sort of penance, I was soon covered in mud and sweat and gore, cradling shattered bodies, listening to cries agonized or terrified, in a world where nothing mattered but the men I was striving to keep alive. I returned from the Vietnam War to The World out of balance, only to find my grandfather in similar shape.

He despaired of America. Everything in America was changing. He took it personally.

His daughter, for whom he silently, stoically still grieved, was dead. His wife, my grandmother, was slipping away from him into dementia, even as he struggled to care for her, to pay for her treatment, to be without her. His troubled grandson had knocked himself off kilter.

He had lived his life confident in his physical presence, but his body was failing him—his heart beat irregularly, sometimes even erratically, and his lungs, stiffened from years of smoking Camels, had him struggling for breath after even mild exertion. A steak-and-potato diet added excess pounds and dangerously elevated his cholesterol levels. His eyesight and hearing dimmed.

He was becoming, in his country and community and family and person, a stranger.

A few months after I returned to Reno for good, I buried him.

Little remained of Chet Stander other than my memories. An old bookcase from our apartment over the bail-bonds office. The two photographs on the table beside my chair. And, in my office, in the locked desk drawer, in an old teakwood box, his .38 Smith and Wesson.

THIRTEEN

The wind woke me, rattling the lid of the old trash can at the back of the house. Still half asleep, I lay listening but heard no more—not the bang of metal, not the sough of the wind, nothing. Because, I came slowly to realize, the wind wasn't blowing.

Now fully awake, I slipped out of bed and into jeans and shoes. In the dark, I found my way to my office and my grandfather's gun. I took it to the patio door, which I slid open carefully.

But not carefully enough. The garbage lid rattled again, sharply. Footsteps thudded. By the time I got around the house to the reek of gasoline, he was gone. In the distance, a car door slammed, an engine roared to life.

I turned on the patio floodlights. A red gas can lay tipped on its side below the window of my guest room. I set it upright and screwed on the lid and then, shivering in the cold, hosed away the spilled gasoline, switched off the outside light, and stepped back inside.

Jittery with fatigue and adrenaline, I knew I wouldn't sleep. I sat in my chair and thought about Rollo Kohler and why he would want to set fire to my house and, no doubt, myself. I was pretty sure he'd torched Merle Stafford's storage barn, on behalf of his grandfather sending Stafford "a message." Now he was after me. I wasn't too concerned for myself, but a sociopath like Rollo might try to get at me through others, Frank or Alicia. I'd have to do something about him.

I let it go, picked up *The Troubled Man*, and tried to read, but Mankell's morose mediation on decline was too close to my own concerns. I gave it up, went back to bed and, eventually, to sleep.

I AWOKE AGAIN at midmorning, still sore, still tired. Forgoing a workout, I stretched a little, dawdled over breakfast and coffee, and thought again about Rollo Kohler. My stupidity with him had had consequences other than my broken hand.

When I eventually got the day going, I drove the rented Lexus to the Subaru dealership, where I kicked some tires as I talked with a salesman. He showed me specs and photos. The package I thought I wanted wasn't on the lot but would arrive in a week or so. I gave him a check and told him to call me when it did.

A car belonging to his youngest son was parked in front of Frank's garage. I didn't stop. And there was no sign of life at Alicia's. So far as I could tell, which it seemed wasn't very far these days, neither place was being watched, and I wasn't followed by either Paulie Hauberk or Rollo Kohler.

A few minutes after I got home, Merle Stafford's pickup pulled in beneath the mulberry tree. I invited him in, gave him coffee. Newt was meeting Carlotta Farragut Ragatz for lunch, he said, not at Emile's but at a Denny's near the airport. Hearing that, I laughed.

Stafford sat at the edge of the sofa, tense, his wiry body coiled. "What's she want, Ross?"

"I don't know, Gunny," I said. "To keep the Ragatz name alive, I'd guess—as if anybody but her cared about it. Maybe she wants to see if Newt's the sort she can make use of."

"She never showed any interest before," he said. He shifted uneasily, coughed. "Why now, when everybody's asking about Howie?"

I shrugged, said again, "I don't know."

"Yeah," he nodded, as if to add his ignorance to mine. "You having any luck looking for that girl's father?"

"I'm waiting for a DNA test result," I said. "If it doesn't come through, well, I'm pretty much out of possibilities."

"And Howie? I mean, I know you ain't actually trying to find him, but I thought, you know, maybe . . ."

"No," I said.

He coughed, for a moment seemed in pain. Then he looked around the room, at the CDs and books and photos. "About the other day—I'm sorry I blew up. It's just that . . ." Suddenly, astonishingly, his eyes filled with tears. "We're losing her."

He hadn't been completely honest with me earlier. His wife's condition was more serious than he'd let on. Doctors didn't quite know how to diagnose Laurel Stafford, but her depression was now complicated by something like dementia. She lived, more and more, in her dreams. She seemed to think that Merle had built her a house that she'd seen in a ladies' magazine when she was a little girl, and she had come rarely to leave it, instead drifting ghostlike through her days, tidying rooms already neat, wiping and brushing already clean surfaces, and preparing pretty meals, oblivious to the world, removed further and further from meaningful relations with her husband and son.

"She's . . . it's like watching somebody disappear, or die."

"I'm sorry. I know it's hard," I said. I glanced at the photograph on the table beside me, at the still smile of the woman who had been so quiet that no one noticed, for some while, that she had gone silent. "My grandmother had Alzheimer's."

"We manage all right, me and Newt," he said. "It's just that if something should happen to me, it'd be all on him. He's great with her, but he'd be alone, and he'd still have to make a living, he wouldn't have a lot of time."

I wasn't sure I understood. "And you're afraid that Carlotta Ragatz will . . . what? Distract him? Come between him and his mother?"

"She hates Laurel," he grunted, again as if in pain. "Always has. She thinks maybe her husband slept with Laurel when she was married to Howie. When Laurel was trying to find money for Howie's bail, she went to their house. Had Newt with her, just a little guy. Maybe that was it too—Laurel had a Ragatz son and Carlotta don't. Wouldn't let her in. Said nasty things."

I considered telling him that Bryce Ragatz had admitted his failure to seduce his cousin's wife—now Merle's wife. I didn't.

"Newt needs to stay as far away from that snarky bitch and her husband as he can get," he said. "Besides, he's got his own problems."

He didn't mean the limp. He meant the constant caution, the wandering off, the flare-ups into violence. He meant that Newt Ragatz was one of those not completely returned from war.

"He loves his mother," I said. "He wouldn't let any harm come to her."

"I know." He stared bleakly into his coffee cup.

I was still confused. "Anyhow, Gunny, why wouldn't you be around? Unless you've got some medical issue?"

"Can't shake this cold, the cough," he said. "Otherwise I'm fine. But you never know, do you? Guy's our age, one day we're here, the next we ain't."

Guys our age.

I didn't know quite what he was telling me—if he was telling me anything. If he was even telling me the truth.

Then, for no apparent reason, he said, "You ever feel guilty, Ross? About Nam, I mean?"

The question set me back in my chair. Veterans of Vietnam, at least the ones I knew, didn't talk about guilt. We'd fought honorably, mostly. We'd followed lawful orders, mostly. Those who would condemn us hadn't been there.

I'd done what I had to do to keep my men whole and alive. As many as I could.

I'd done my duty, as best I could.

Except of course it wasn't that simple. We always knew, some of us, that we would have to go back to The World, where we would be held, unfairly we thought, accountable. And we always knew that in The World we would be found at least lacking. But we always knew too, from the moment that we stepped into the wet and fetid Southeast Asian air, that our country had broken trust with us.

I felt guilty only because I'd survived, when many better men than I had not.

"I can live with what I did, Gunny."

He looked past me. "Yeah. Me too, even though I never did much. But the Corps made killing easier. Obey orders, do your job, don't think. Now . . ."

I waited. He was about to say something. Then he put down his coffee cup and rose. "Thanks for the coffee."

I walked him to his pickup. He looked over the Lexus. "New car?"

"Rental," I said. I told him what had happened on Mount Rose Highway. As he listened, he absently rubbed a film of desert grime from the Corps decal on his rear window.

"This Rollo is Joe Kohler's grandson? He tried to kill you?"

"He came around last night too, with a gas can in his hand and arson on his mind. I can't prove it, of course," I said. "The same way you can't actually prove who set your barn on fire."

His look told me I was right.

"Joe Kohler called," Stafford said, angry now. "Thought we had money Howie stole. Years ago, he'd come around, looking for Howie and money then too, but I told him to fuck off. Anyhow, he called a while back and made threats, and then the barn got torched. He's in a wheelchair, so he hired it done, I figured. Didn't know about the grandson."

"And now Joe's dead," I said. "Somebody beat him to death with a tire iron."

"Breaks my heart," he said.

I didn't say anything.

He smiled a small angry smile, with a sharp harsh scrape cleared his throat. "If I wanted to kill Joe Kohler, I'd of done it years ago."

It came out then. A week or so after Howie Ragatz's disappearance, Kohler insisting that Laurel must know where her husband was. Putting his hands on her. It wasn't rape, but it might have been if Merle Stafford hadn't appeared. Combat Marine versus bar brawler. No contest.

"I told that fucker if I ever seen him again, I'd kill him. Then a year or so ago I come on him in Walmart, all knotted up, in a wheelchair. Wouldn't have been worth the effort."

"It could have been Maglie," I said, "Or one of his goons. But Joe's dead, and Rollo's beef with me is personal, so your part in this is finished. Whatever this is."

"You don't know?"

"No, but I think it's about over." Events—deaths, revelations—seemed to be shaping themselves toward crisis and conclusion. Or maybe I just wished it to be so.

"Yeah." he said. He opened the door to his pickup, and as he slid inside he gave me that same small angry smile. "Semper Fi, Marine."

I watched him drive away. I wasn't sure why he'd come. What had he to do with Bryce Ragatz, if anything? Why would someone kill Joe Kohler? How did Len Maglie fit into whatever was going on? Things didn't add up. Or maybe I was just too old to do basic arithmetic anymore.

But I was also disturbed. Our talk of Vietnam had dredged up old feelings, confusions. War brought us together, the marines of Mike Three Five, as we fought not for our country but for each other. Our country, we often felt, gave no thought to us. We had been sent to war and forgotten. Deserted.

Now I poured another cup of coffee, sat in my chair, and remembered.

One rainy night, I led a squad into a darkness that obliterated the trail we could follow only by the feel of bare firm earth underfoot. At a bend, we set up an ambush. My men were trained and practiced, quick, quiet, sure. We settled into our positions to wait for the enemy.

In the darkness, we couldn't see one another. We could hear only the spat of rain on jungle leaves. We could smell the rot of vegetation and the reek of our own bodies.

The rain came harder. Then slowly the darkness changed, became an absence. I knew then that the enemy would not be coming down the trail. They had gone, fled. In the jungle night, we were alone.

I got on the radio and whispered a call. The receiver crackled, but no one spoke. I called again. Static.

Rain spattered. The night smelled of death. The darkness was impenetrable.

We had been abandoned.

I'd never forgotten that moment. Even though, after a long silent while, we made our way back to the company, where I discovered that the radio receiver was faulty. But almost from the day of my return to The World, I couldn't say whether I was remembering an experience or a dream.

Now I had a similar sense of having been left. My mother and grandparents were dead. My friend was dying, and I no longer had a wife, and my daughter was several hundred miles away, immersed in her own life. Such losses were merely part of life, I knew, but the knowledge did not console me.

But I didn't have time to dwell on it. My phone rang. Frank had news.

Preparing to leave the house, I thought about taking along my grandfather's gun, even though I had no real reason to. I wanted things over, ended.

I left the pistol where it was.

"YOU LOOK LIKE a raccoon."

The jest came to cover my shock. Frank's eyes were bulged and darkly ringed, his face a pasty white. He slumped in the doorway. He breathed in shallow gasps.

"You know a red crew-cab pickup? It's been checking out the neighborhood. Alicia's seen him too."

"Rollo Kohler," I said. "You need to be careful with him, Frank. He's not too bright, but he's big and he's mean. He likes to set fires and to hurt people."

"Big and mean I can handle," he said, panting.

I didn't think he could handle much of anything, but I didn't say so. I followed him to the kitchen. He poured us coffee.

"The autopsy on Joe Kohler isn't complete or official," he said, "but cause of death will be a broken neck."

I hadn't actually expected that, but it didn't surprise me. "Maybe the C2 vertebra?"

He frowned. "How did you know?"

"And the battering with the tire iron was postmortem," I said. "To cover it up, so the cops won't connect it to Gale Dunn, who also died of a neck fracture."

"That makes it a new ball game," he said evenly. "You'll be passing on this information to the appropriate law-enforcement officials, of course."

"Not yet," I said. "At this point I don't actually *know* anything. Her death is officially an accident; his, a brutal murder. There's a connection, but it's tenuous."

Frank scowled but said nothing. His eyes were rheumy, glistening. His raspy breathing sounded painful.

I was concerned. "Are you sure you're all right?"

"Yeah," he said, but without conviction. He looked out the patio door at Paltry, crossed sticks and black cloth and wizened fruit. "I'm seeing the cardiologist this afternoon. More pills, probably, and advice on clean living."

That last was ironic. Frank had never smoked or done drugs of any kind, drank only wine with dinner and the occasional beer, and kept himself in shape. None of that mattered now, it seemed.

I couldn't help but feel fortunate. I'd been banged up a bit recently, had a sore head and liver and hand and knee, and I wasn't immune to the twinges and aches of age, but I suffered no serious health problems. This despite dissolute decades once I returned from Vietnam. Neither of my grandparents had lived to my age, but I had good genes from my father, it seemed, whoever he might have been.

Frank seemed to sense what I was thinking. "As they say, getting old ain't for sissies."

"As they also say, it beats the alternative."

"I'm not so sure about that." After a pause, he said, "It's tricky, snapping a neck, not like in the movies. Takes skill, and strong hands. We know anybody made his reputation with his hands?"

"Yeah," I said. "But why would Maglie do it himself? Why not one of his stooges?"

"For the fun of it?" Frank scowled. "Show the young Turks he's still got it? But the real question is why he'd want them dead. An alcoholic ex-erotic dancer and a stove-up old thug."

"It's got to be the money." I told him what Bryce Ragatz had told me about the robbery and his cousin's part in it. "You were right about that. But Maglie isn't being forthright about why he thinks it's his money that's missing."

"It seems to me," Frank said, "if he's looking for missing money, he'd want to keep everybody involved alive, at least till he found it."

That made sense.

He sagged, as if to fold in on himself. This conversation was taking a lot out of him. "It also seems to me that he's making a big fuss over not all that much. A quarter of a million is serious money, but is it enough to kill two people over?"

"Maybe," I said. "I don't know what to think. Not that it matters. The only thing I care about is identifying Mia Dunn's father."

"Anything new?"

I told him about Bryce Ragatz's admission and the sweatband. "I should know today or tomorrow."

"You think he's the one?"

"More like hope," I said. "If not, I'm out of candidates. We don't have any of Randy's DNA, so that's a dead end. If it isn't Bryce Ragatz, we'll probably never learn who it is."

"My sister won't be happy."

"I won't be happy either," I said. "I wanted to be able to do this for her."

He nodded. "How's that going, the two of you."

I had to think about it. "We're trying."

FOURTEEN

Good Beans was busy—a trio of skateboarders, an amorous teenage couple, a woman working on a laptop, hospital staff filling a table. Mia Dunn was seated again in the center of the room. She watched my approach, saying, as I sat, "You've found out something? About my father?"

"Not yet."

Her face fell. "I know," she said dispiritedly, "the chances aren't good. But . . ."

"I'm sorry the Howie Ragatz thing didn't work out," I said. "I know you would have liked Newt to be your brother."

She smiled through her disappointment. "That would have been nice. But we can still be—we still are friends. We . . . talk."

Mia's brief pause had been laden with possibilities. Her gaze slid, rested briefly on the lovers, the girl a slender dishwater blonde whose white throat arched as her tattooed and pony-tailed boyfriend nuzzled her nape. Mia reluctantly turned back to me.

"I'm tying up some loose ends," I said. "I've seen the official reports on your mother's death. She'd had an awful lot to drink."

She nodded. "I told you, didn't I? That last year, she was bad."

"What was she was doing up on the tractor?" I registered her frown, pushed on. "It was the middle of the night. Her blood alcohol was so high, she must have been in a near-stupor. The tractor was parked facing into the shed, so she would have been sitting there in the dark staring at a wall," I said. "I know it's not difficult, getting up onto one of those things, but still, and more important, why would she?"

"You said on the phone you wanted to talk about her death," she said uncertainly. "I don't know how I can help. I mean, I wasn't there."

"Who would want to hurt her? Did she have any real enemies?"

Mia's eyes widened. "You think . . . ?"

"I don't know what to think, for sure," I said. "That's why I'm asking."

She sat back in her chair. She looked again at the teenage lovers, now leaning together as if asleep or dead. "Everybody was her enemy."

As she had the day we met, Mia spoke of her mother with difficulty, distressed, repeating what she had heard, what she had witnessed. Gale Dunn was an only child, at once spoiled and oppressed. In school, she was intelligent but lazy and willful. Entering puberty, she decided that she was special—why else would men watch her as they did? The admonitions of her mother she dismissed, the dictates of her father she defied. At sixteen, she ran off.

"She and my granddad, he was strict, and she wanted . . . *more*, I guess. More than just a hay farm." The young woman smiled sadly. "Which is what she ended up with."

Gale Dunn's parents, when she left, reported her gone but did not look for her. She came back a couple of times, briefly, wanting money, which she didn't get. Then her father died, and a bit later she returned with a child, and she stayed, she worked and drank and grew angrier and angrier and she took out her anger on whoever she happened to encounter, irritating and alienating everyone she knew, and she waited. Alone. With death in her head.

Once again, I found myself, for no clear reason, feeling something like sympathy for Gale Dunn.

"She was waiting for him," Mia said. "For Howie Ragatz, it has to be. The photograph on her bedtable, I mean . . ."

"And all those years," I prompted, "she had no friends, no men in her life, no—"

"All she had was me," Mia said, "and she hated me. She *abused* me. She didn't hit me or anything, I'm not saying that, but she was never warm or affectionate, never nurturing. She looked at me and I could see it, the hate. She looked at me, and I cried."

She was crying now, or nearly, her green eyes wet and glistening.

"I didn't—I don't know why. What had I done? Why did my just being there make her mad? Why did she have to be mean to me, and ugly, and cold? Why couldn't she love me, even a little?"

Her childlike voice had roughened as she seemed to plead with her dead mother. She was for that moment younger than her years, a little girl again.

I didn't know what to say. She needed help, but I certainly wasn't qualified to give it. "Have you ever talked to anyone about this, Mia? Counselors? Therapists?"

"All through high school," she said. From her bag she took a tissue, dabbed at the corner of her eye. "College too. It helped." She dampened the tissue. I waited. She recovered. "Are you saying that somebody murdered my mother?"

"I think your mother's death isn't as simple as the authorities have it," I said. "I think it might be connected to things that happened years ago, before you were born. Your mother, over her last year, when she got drunk and made nasty phone calls to people she used to know—I think she said the wrong thing to the wrong person."

She listened with obvious bewilderment. "Is this about the man you warned us about? The hoodlum?"

"He's involved," I said. "There are others. But I don't know if I know them all. I hoped you might be able to tell me."

"Who she called?" She shook her head. "The only one I know is Tabby, but you already talked to her. We were going to go see her, Newt and I. He wants to help me." A small smile softened her features. Her voice went wistful.

Newton Ragatz and Mia Dunn. Maybe this was just her wishing, but maybe it was more.

"I have to go, but . . ." She rose, frowned, then whispered, "The way she looked at me, Tabby? I think she saw something, somebody. I think she knows."

She turned to gaze once more at the amorous young couple. She nearly spoke. Instead, she gave them a sad smile and made her way out into the daylight.

After Mia left, I ordered a latte, nursed it as the place slowly emptied, until only I and the lovebirds remained. A phrase my grandmother would have used, "Lovebirds." Was it still current? Did young people bill-and-coo? Probably not. Who even remembered the terms—only old farts like me, old and out of it.

And basically useless. I had nowhere to go, nothing to do, really, until I heard from the DNA lab. Because, I had to remind myself once again, I was trying to establish Mia Dunn's paternity. And, I hoped, Randy Barnes's fidelity. That was all. Nevertheless.

I was persuaded, on the basis of no evidence whatsoever, that in a drunken phone call Gale Dunn had said something that someone found threatening. That someone had silenced her. That same someone, for reasons that I didn't know, had killed and silenced Joe Kohler as well. And all this had to do with Howie Ragatz robbing his cousin Bryce of money that Len Maglie insisted belonged to him.

Gale Dunn had called Bryce Ragatz, spoken to his wife, and accused Bryce of killing Howie Ragatz. She had called Laurel Stafford, but the calls had been intercepted by first her son, who listened to the drunken woman accuse his mother of killing his father, and then by her husband. She had called Joe Kohler, accusing him of killing Howie in a fight over the robbery money, and then urging him to kill Merle and Laurel Stafford. And she called Tabby Sabich, accusing "somebody" of killing Howie.

Now I wondered if Gale Dunn hadn't also called Len Maglie. What could she have said that would threaten him? That he was somehow involved in the armed robbery, for which there was in Nevada no statute of limitations?

Had she also called Alicia Barnes? I thought it likely. But what had she said? I didn't want to know. I hoped I wouldn't need to. I hoped that Bryce Ragatz's DNA would answer the question both Alicia and Mia had asked, so that I could get back to my life. Such as it was.

The lovers untangled and, in a daze, departed. I wasn't far behind them.

As I stepped out into the afternoon, a man rose from his squat at the rear end of my rented Lexus. His flattop and square jaw made him look like a concrete block. And I understood something.

"You put a bug on my car," I said. "You just pick me up from time to time, and with the GPS you don't need to get close and show yourself."

Paulie Hauberk said nothing.

"I don't suppose you were at my place last night."

He still said nothing.

"Last night," I repeated, "when Rollo Kohler tried to burn down my house?"

His mouth moved, barely. "Persistent, ain't he?"

I took that as a no. "He's probably the one who ran me off the road. Thanks for the help with that."

He shrugged. I'd wondered why he'd troubled himself with me up on the mountain. It seemed he wasn't going to tell me.

As he turned to step over to his SUV, I said, "I've been thinking about a couple of things, Paulie. Like, when you were driving Bryce Ragatz and his money around, who were you working for, Harvey Prior or Len Maglie?"

"The boss," he said. Harvey Prior, he meant.

"And then when Maglie became boss?"

"I work for him."

"And when Snooks becomes boss?"

That provoked a reaction. Not much of one, a deep breath, a tensing of his eyebrows, but enough to encourage me.

"I'm trying to figure out why Maglie says the money that got your hand shot off belongs to him. And why Snooks wants to know all about it. Is Snooks maybe trying to get something on Maglie, so he can push him out the way Maglie shoved out Harvey Prior?"

This was a new idea to Paulie. He didn't like it.

"Somebody engineered the robbery, Paulie. Howie Ragatz led the guys in the alley, but somebody told him where and when and why to hit Bryce Ragatz. And you. Who could that have been?"

Paulie didn't answer. I was about to give it up when he said, "Don't mess with Snooks. He's too good. You're too old."

"I don't intend to mess with anybody," I said.

"Did you kill him?"

It took me a moment. "Oh, Rollo, last night. No."

"Should of." He did smile then, barely.

"The guy who blew away your hand," I said. "His name was Joe Kohler. Rollo's grandfather. I didn't kill him either, but somebody did."

Something shifted behind his eyes. Then he nodded. "Thanks."

I watched him leave. Then I left too. I went home and took a nap.

I slept hard, awoke unrefreshed and cranky. My mood didn't improve as I fought rush-hour traffic to Sparks and the Lemon Tree Apartments. I pressed the bell button repeatedly. At last the door edged open, allowing Tabby Sabich to peer at me through a narrow crack. Weakly, even meekly, she said, "Go away."

"You can let me in to chat," I said, "or I can ring this bell till the cows come home."

"I don't know what you think I can tell you." She tried to sneer but couldn't pull it off. I thought she might be ill.

I pressed the doorbell.

At last she drew back the door. She wasn't wearing her cat's-eye spectacles, so her face seemed bare, infant-pudgy and doll-like. Her muumuu was splattered with jungle colors, greens and blues and yellows and oranges. As before, I followed her halting step through the office into the room with the overstuffed furniture and the wall of photographs. We sat.

"You're not well," I said.

"I hurt," she said, "Veins, knees, feet. You spend the best years your body's got dancing night after night for drunks and assholes and see how you feel twenty-five years later."

Speaking, she'd turned to the wall of photographs, seeming to seek reassurance that her body's best years had actually occurred.

"Why did you?" I asked.

She paused, as if before a question that had never occurred to her. "I wanted to dance. That's all I ever wanted. I took lessons, worked hard, I could have been good, could have danced in the casino shows, if I hadn't . . ." Her lips pursed into a bitter pout. "I was so stupid. I thought I could breeze into the Blue Flame and make some money and then . . ."

She let the thought go, or seemed to. Then she went on, "And now I'm fat and hurting. I always had to fight the weight thing. Then after a while, I just let it happen, I—I was getting to the end. I mean, after a certain age the body starts to lump and sag, and young girls are always slinking in, if a person doesn't make some kind of move she ends up . . ."

She didn't want to think about where a person ends up, if she's working in a place like the Blue Flame or Off Limits—on the dancer-hooker circuit that was actually a spiral, downward.

"How did you end up here?"

"With all this, you mean?" She managed a sneer. "I was loyal, did what I was told, made myself useful. And I got protection."

"That would be the Max Brand fan," I said, nodding at the books still on the lamp table.

She waved a fat hand. "Hey, he's all right. Treats me like I'm a person. And it's better than stripping in jerk-off parlors or giving blow jobs in some falling-down whorehouse."

Despite her discomfort, she was perking up some. I decided to make a run at her.

"Mia Dunn thinks you know who her father was."

"She can think what she wants," Tabby said. "Doesn't make it so."

"What did Gale Dunn say when she called you?"

Tabby shook her head. "She was so drunk she could hardly say anything. Tried to have it that everybody killed Howie Ragatz. Everybody being, I guess, Harvey and Len and Bryce Ragatz and the Barnes guy, even me and Paulie."

"Which one of them killed her?"

That knocked her off balance. Her baby-doll mouth opened and closed like a gasping carp's. "Killed her? I thought she had an accident."

"Tell me about Gale and Bryce Ragatz."

"Nothing to tell. Like I said before, he come sniffing around, yeah. Far as them getting together, who knows?"

"When you first saw Mia Dunn, who did she remind you of?"

"It's just . . . she's sort of plain," Tabby said. "I mean, her mother was good-looking, and you'd think her daughter might . . . but I really don't know anybody who looks like her."

I was getting nowhere.

"The fuss between Randy Barnes and Howie Ragatz—tell me about that."

"Male pissing contest," she scoffed. "Barnes had a thing for Gale, he thought he saw something in her . . . told her he could help her get out of the Blue Flame, wanted her to think she could go to school, be something better than what she was. Stupid bastard. He didn't get it. Girls like me and Gale, we could leave when and if Harvey Prior said. And then Len Maglie."

"And Howie?"

"Barnes thought Howie was the reason she stayed at the Blue Flame, waiting for him to dump his wife. Barnes, he was stuck on her, but Gale just messed with him. Then she was pregnant and Maglie took over and Howie disappeared and Gale had her kid and went home."

"And she never told you, then or later, who Mia's father was?"

The fat old ex-dancer shook her head. "All I know is once she was pregnant, she was working some kind of scam, her and Howie, trying to pin the kid on somebody. I don't know who. But it didn't work, so it doesn't matter, I guess."

Except, I thought, that it had worked.

"What do you think happened to Howie Ragatz," I asked.

"He's dead," she said. "Somebody killed him."

"Who?"

She looked again at the wall of photos, and the past, as if she was after a way out of the present, a way to avoid the question. "I don't know."

"Sure you do." Because she was afraid to say even whom she suspected. And there was only one person she was afraid of these days. "Len Maglie."

"No," she said, a bit too loudly. "He was looking for Howie, hard. Still is."

That was true. But I still thought I was right. I let it go.

"He had this smile," she said. "It wasn't a grin or anything, it was this little smile, like he knew. Like he knew who you really were."

She was remembering Howie Ragatz. "And Gale? Mia said her mother wanted more."

"Except she didn't know more of what," Tabby said. "Even so, she could convince you she deserved it."

As I thought about that, a man stepped into the room. Tabby Sabich's smile said he wasn't a threat. He was the opposite: her protection. The Max Brand fan.

"Dinner time," Paulie Hauberk said.

I stood. "*Bon appetit*. I'll show myself out."

FIFTEEN

I spent an uneasy evening, trying to read Mankell, not really listening to Sinatra and The Mamas and The Poppas and Patsy Cline, and brooding about Rollo Kohler: where was he, what was he doing or planning, how was I going to deal with him? I didn't like the thought of him hanging around Frank's neighborhood and Alicia's Caughlin Ranch home. I'd have to do something about it, and soon.

I was thinking too, as I had earlier that day, of my grandmother. Something like Laurel Stafford, she had faced life with a small smile, behind which she'd lived alone. At her grave, her husband of nearly a half-century acknowledged that he never really knew her. Her daughter, I came to learn, had believed her incapable of serious thought, feeling, or aspiration. To me, she was always there but never near. I knew she loved me, but only with the part of her that smiled.

She lived yet in my memory, in the smell of Jergen's hand lotion, which she applied each evening after washing the dinner dishes; in the taste of the buttery cookies she baked each Saturday morning; in the sight of puffy cumulus clouds like those that patterned the cloth of her faded favorite robe. I was probably the only person left alive to ever give Meta Ammonson Stander a thought. Soon I too would pass, and she.

I was sunk in such cheerful ruminations when the phone rang.

It was Alicia.

Frank was in the hospital. He would undergo a triple bypass the next morning.

She had driven him to his appointment with the cardiologist, who took one look at him and called an ambulance.

She had phoned his sons, all of whom had been to see him and would be back in the morning.

Frank was medicated and sleeping.

Alicia sounded exhausted.

The next morning, we met in the hallway outside Frank's room.

The operation had been successful but would have little long-term effect. Frank's heart was worn out, his lungs were filling with fluid, and his kidneys were barely functioning. Death, the young surgeon said, was inevitable but not necessarily imminent.

Alicia was not taking it well, now angry, now aggrieved, now despondent. Late in the morning, I enticed her from her sleeping brother's bedside down to the Renown Starbuck's. Approaching our table, her double tall mocha and my own latte in hand, I saw with a shock how she had aged. Her seated body bent as if under the weight of care and years. Her hair was ropy and lusterless, her face a sag of flesh on bone. Her eyes, red-rimmed and shimmery, looked sore and blank.

"You should go home and get some rest," I said, sitting.

She'd slept little the night before, then arrived at the hospital before Frank was wheeled into surgery, and she'd sat with his sons through the bypass procedure and after.

"I can't," she said quietly.

Nor could I, not until I knew he was out of danger. "I know."

"That inevitable but not imminent guff," she said sharply. "Does that mean he doesn't know? That he's just covering his ass?"

"Probably," I said.

Her annoyance turned to anguish. "Frank is up there dying."

All I could think of to say was that we were all dying. But she would take no comfort in such a remark, would probably hear it as a smart-ass quip, which it probably was, just me trying to stay in balance. I kept my mouth shut.

"I want to go to Italy."

This came without preamble, perhaps because she knew I'd heard it before. Both sets of her grandparents were from Umbria. Her maternal grandfather, a bocce-ball fanatic, and her paternal grandmother, given to muttering imprecations in Italian while at Mass and meals, had attended our wedding. Alicia even then had talked about someday going over to the Old Country.

"Randy was going to take me on our anniversary," she said. "The first one was the tenth, I think. Then the twentieth, and the twenty-fifth, but something always came up."

I had also pledged to take her to Italy. Another promise broken. She didn't remind me of it, perhaps had forgotten.

"I want to sell the house too." She leaned back in her chair. "It's too big for me. I don't entertain much anymore, and Randy . . . he's dead. I have to let him go."

Again I had nothing to say.

"I don't mean forget him." As if I'd accused her of perfidy, she angrily went on. "I don't mean that. I mean just let him be dead. Keep him as a memory, not as a presence."

"I understand," I said.

"I could let him go, I mean, if I knew . . . why haven't you found out—or are you even trying?" Her voice had risen in pitch and volume. "My friends, I know you haven't talked to any of them. What have you been doing? You promised me, you promised—" She caught, controlled herself. "I need to know, Jack."

I told her, quietly, what I could. "Everyone I've spoken with doubts that Randy ever went to bed with Gale Dunn. He liked her, saw something of value in her, and he was trying to help her, to get her out of sex clubs. But they weren't lovers. Her lover was Howie Ragatz."

That didn't satisfy her. "But you don't know for sure that they didn't sleep together, once anyhow?"

"I don't know anything for sure, Alicia," I said, suddenly tired, sore, old. "It was a long time ago, and it's part of a complicated mess, robbery and drugs and murder."

That seemed not to have registered. "So that girl isn't Randy's daughter?"

I couldn't say that. "I'm waiting for the results of another DNA test. That might settle the matter. If it doesn't, well . . ."

She raised her mocha, drank. Her hand trembled. She was upset, afflicted by anger, sorrow, uncertainty. Her eyes glistened again with tears.

For a moment I remained silent, debating. I didn't want to add to her unhappiness. But I needed to ask the question I didn't want to know the answer to.

"Did you, within the last year, get a late-night phone call? From a woman? Drunk?"

Alicia went wide-eyed. "How did you know?"

"Gale Dunn called several people. I'm trying to find out what she said."

Apprehension swept aside her anger. "I should have told you, but . . . I got it on my machine. She said she and Randy had been involved. She accused him of killing Howie Ragatz. Over her."

There it was, finally. "Is that what you really wanted me to find out, Alicia? If Randy killed Howie Ragatz?"

"No, no. I mean . . ." Alicia again composed herself. "Did he? Randy? Kill him?"

"No," I said. But that wasn't enough. "I mean, I can't be sure. But I'm sure."

Then her eyes widened in discovery. "But by *involved*, she didn't mean sex, did she? It was that business with Bryce Ragatz's accounts. She got Randy to do it, didn't she? To steal the money."

That might have been right. Infatuated, Randy would have been susceptible, seducible. Maybe it was sex. Maybe it was just setting things right. If Gale Dunn had told him that Bryce Ragatz sired her unborn child, she might have persuaded Randy to make certain that Ragatz bore the financial burden of fatherhood. "I think so."

Alicia drank more coffee. "Tell me about her. Gale Dunn. The woman in the photograph."

I told her what I could. The alfalfa farm. The young girl who thought she must be special because of the way men looked at her. The sixteen-year-old runaway. The Blue Flame dancer and boss's favorite. The abandoned lover. The angry mother. The crazy woman who made midnight phone calls. The middle-aged drunk who died not of a stroke made inescapable by a malformation in her brain but, officially at least, from falling off a tractor.

Alicia sat silent, her eyelids lowered, so still she might have been sleeping. Her makeup looked like crayon smeared on cardboard. When she finally spoke, it was bitterly. "You like her."

"She was a horrible woman, in a lot of ways," I said.

"You sympathize." She snapped open her eyes. "She's just like your mother!"

I started to protest, caught myself.

I had to acknowledge the similarities. Both attracted men, had trouble with their fathers, had run off as teenagers, had been dancers of a sort. Wanted more. It was a comparison I'd need time and different circumstances to work through.

Now we sat silently in the hospital coffee shop, surrounded by aides and orderlies and nurses and families and visitors, an old man and an old woman who were once, briefly, long ago, a couple.

"I'm sorry," Alicia said eventually.

"You might be right. In a way."

"But I shouldn't have said." She offered a small repentant smile. "It was cruel."

"No harm done," I granted.

My phone rang. The technician at the DNA lab said that Mia Dunn's father was not Bryce Ragatz. I told Alicia.

"That leaves only Randy, doesn't it," she said, calm now.

"No," I said. "It might have been Harvey Prior. Or a friend of his he handed her over to for a couple of hours. And . . ." I was thinking then of Len Maglie, of what he'd said. "I have one more lead to pursue."

She grimaced. "I'm sorry I brought you into this, Jack. I'm sorry I didn't just throw the note from Mia Dunn in the trash. I mean, what difference does it make, really? He was my husband and I loved him, no matter what he did."

This was precisely the opposite of what she had said a few minutes before. But both could be true. If Randy Barnes had broken faith with her, then their marriage hadn't been as solid as she'd always thought. But Randy was dead and what had happened a quarter of a century before was of no real consequence now.

I walked her back to the Intensive Care Unit. Frank should have been conscious by now but wasn't. The doctors weren't certain why. Alicia relieved Frank's watching son and resumed her bedside vigil.

I left her there.

The desert looked drab, lifeless. The sun gave weak light and no heat. The world seemed tired. So, as I drove, I projected my mood.

I parked behind Merle Stafford's pickup. The retired gunnery sergeant stood at the edge of the blackened rectangle once the floor of the old barn. In the far corner was a patch of lighter colored earth. A hole had been dug, refilled, and tamped down.

"Looking for something, Gunny?"

"Might put up another structure here," he said. "I thought if there was a foundation, we could use it. Dug around yesterday. No such luck."

Something didn't seem right, but I didn't pursue it. "I wanted to check with Newt, see what Carlotta Ragatz had to say."

"He's in the shop," Stafford said. "Go on in. I'll be there in a minute."

He glanced at the house. A white face floated in a window. Laurel Stafford looked out at us. Or past us, to the desert. Her husband raised his hand in a gentle wave. She didn't respond.

In the shop, Newt Ragatz was hand-sanding a cabinet door. He stopped his work and offered me coffee. I took a stool at a workbench. "How'd it go yesterday?"

In his quiet, careful way he told me about his lunch with Carlotta

Farragut Ragatz. She'd asked about his past and his prospects but hadn't been especially interested in his responses. She spoke of Howie Ragatz, of his facile charm and unfortunate habits, of his trouble with the law, and of his great desire to be included in the family of Carl Ragatz, hinting that such might be possible for Newt, should he and she "get along." She also inquired of Laurel's past, insinuating that as a cocktail waitress she would have been dependent on the tips and favors of lustful men; that her claim that she was pregnant by Howie Ragatz had never been confirmed by a blood test; and that after Howie disappeared she'd taken up with an older man and retreated to the desert, which could be so very lonely for a woman used to masculine attention.

Despite my own encounter with Carlotta Farragut Ragatz, I was taken aback. "You put up with that?"

"I'll put up with almost anything." His voice was soft, his eyes not. "For a while."

She had asked him what he knew of his father. What had he been told about the relation of cousins Howie and Bryce? Had he ever heard talk about a robbery? Had he ever seen them together, his mother and her husband, had Laurel ever spoken of Bryce Ragatz and their past?

"Their past?" I was confused. "What does that mean?"

"It added up," Newt said. "She wanted to know if Bryce Ragatz was really my father."

"What did you tell her?" I asked.

He smiled a soft, hard-eyed smile. "I told her to go fuck herself."

I laughed.

I was finishing my coffee when we heard a vehicle pull into the lot. A door slammed. Newt stood. "Business."

I followed him out of the shop into the sun. Dust was settling on the red pickup. Rollo Kohler, in a Raiders ball cap, padded orange vest, and camouflage pants, might have been about to set off deer hunting. But not with the pistol in his hand.

"Hold it," he said, straining to snarl. His blue eyes seemed even more out of place in his fat, hairy face. "I'll put a fucking hole in your gut."

I sighed. I was tired. Tired of Rollo Kohler and his dead grandfather, of Len Maglie and his goons. Tired of trying not to be who and what I once was.

I offered him a sneer. "Got your voice back, I see."

"Fuck you." He waived the gun at me. "You killed him, my granddad."

"Why would I want to do that?"

I took a step forward. He jerked the gun barrel at me. I stopped even as Newt, understanding, eased up beside me.

"Why? Why—" He sputtered, confused. I wasn't responding properly. "The money, you fucker, the money."

"Lord, but you're stupid, Rollo." I kept my voice low, insistent. I wanted to confuse and to anger him. "There is no money. And even if there were, Joe didn't know where it was, so why would I kill him? Only an ignoramus would think that."

"Hey, you were at the house." He jabbed the air with his pistol. "Now you tell me where the money is or I'll fucking blow you away."

On a couple of occasions, back in my crazy days, I'd been under another man's gun and I'd laughed. Not out of courage, not bravado. I'd laughed because the situation struck me as absurd. As now: my only real friend was in a hospital, dying, and I was fooling with a fathead with a gun. So I laughed. And Rollo Kohler looked at me, bewildered.

"Nice-looking piece you've got there," I said. "Glock .357, looks like. Too bad I'm going to have to make you eat it."

"You beat-up old fucker, you try it and I'll—"

"You aren't going to do anything," I said, advancing. "You don't shoot people you're facing. You burn barns and houses under the cover of night. You run people off the road. You mug druggies and old ladies, but you let a decrepit old fart like me dump you in the mud." I grinned. "Besides, you shoot me, and Newt here will tear your throat out."

Newt had moved with me. Rollo pointed his gun at him, his gaze skittery, his hand trembling. "I'll fucking put a bullet in you too."

"I don't think so," Newt said slowly, with his soft smile. "You'd have to get us both, and I don't think you could. Especially since you've got the safety on."

Rollo looked. That was all Newt needed. After a sudden flurry of movement, the Glock was in the dust, as was the big man, thrashing in the choke hold of the small young Marine.

I picked up the pistol, checked. The safety wasn't on.

Already Rollo Kohler was struggling less. His eyes were swelling. His mouth sagged into a grimace.

"Nice move," I said. "That's enough. He's finished."

But Newt Ragatz wasn't there. He was in a world where death hid in every snap of twig and swirl of dust in the wind.

"At ease," I said, louder.

The big man's eyes bulged. His mouth gaped. His limbs began to flop.

"At ease!" I yelled, "Stand down!"

A gunshot boomed in the dry desert air. Releasing his hold, Newt Ragatz leaped into a crouch and scanned the lot. Merle Stafford hastened toward us.

"Newt! For Christ's sake!"

Newt started toward his stepfather.

"Stand down, Marine!"

Something in my voice—authority, perhaps, command—finally stopped him. He set himself again in a squat, ready to assault, head swiveling from me to Merle Stafford, who slowed and came up carefully, a big pistol hanging from his hand.

Then slowly, cautiously, Newt straightened up. "Yeah, I got it. I got it."

In the sun and the dust, we three waited for Rollo Kohler to recover. Merle Stafford had seen the big, bearded man covering us with his gun, he said, had retrieved the old .45 he'd kept in a bedside drawer, and had taken it to the porch. He was too far off to shoot, and the space was too open for him to sneak up. Then Newt had made his move. Even from a distance, Merle could tell that Newt was somewhere else. He fired his .45 to jolt him back to reality.

"Good thing, too," I said.

He stuffed the big pistol into his jeans.

Newt said nothing. Like Rollo Kohler, he was recovering. Unlike Rollo Kohler, his recovery would not be complete. Ever.

Finally, Rollo struggled to his feet. We didn't help him. He stood, staggered, wobbled. He waved a hand at me, gave me a petulant look. "That cost me five hundred dollars."

The Glock. He knew he wasn't getting it back.

"The price you pay," I said. "I'm going to destroy this piece, but I've got one of my own. And if you ever bother me, or Frank Calvetti or his sister, or anybody I've even so much as had a cup of coffee with, I'll come after you with it."

"I ain't afraid of you." But he was. Which added to the absurdity. He had fifty pounds and nearly that many years on me.

Warily, he climbed into his pickup and fired it up, revving the engine, as if to reestablish his braggart's sense of self. His back tires spat dirt and dust at us as he sped off.

Newt Ragatz stood still, silent, watching him go. He brushed at the dust on his knees and forearms. "You don't care either, do you?"

At first, I wasn't sure that he was addressing me. Then I saw his eyes. I'd seen those eyes before in Vietnam, in the gaze of war-worn men for whom it made little difference whether they lived or died.

"Sometimes," I said. "Most of the time, I care, I try . . ."

"Yeah," he said. He held out his hand for the pistol. "Can I see it?"

I gave it to him. He tried its feel, heft. "Nice. Mind if I keep it?" He smiled at his stepfather. "If you get to have a gun, I should too, huh?"

I shrugged. Merle Stafford watched his stepson.

"Back to work," Newt said. He slipped the Glock into his pocket. "Semper Fi."

When Newt was inside, Merle Stafford said quietly, "You maybe understand him better than I do. He can't get past it."

"It takes a while."

"It's taken you fifty years," he said, "and you ain't done with it, are you?"

"Maybe not," I said. "It doesn't go away. You just learn to see when it isn't real. He can get help with that, Gunny. The Corps has programs, and the V.A. Without them, I don't know where I'd be. Dead, probably."

"I'll talk to him."

We stood in the puny sunlight. Up on the porch, Laurel Stafford now sat sedately at the small table. Unmoving, she looked down at us. At that distance, she was hardly a presence, more an illusion, a mirage.

After a while I said, "How many times did Gale Dunn phone here, Gunny?"

"Hard to say." He looked past me, out into the desert. He coughed. "The phone would ring late at night. I shut it off before it went to the machine. There for a while, I pulled out the jack when I went to bed. I guess I don't really know."

"You talked to her, didn't you?

"Once," he said, "I didn't talk much. Listened, mostly. Same crap Newt got. Her and Howie were lovers, all set to run off. Me and Laurel killed him."

"Were they?"

"Lovers? Yeah." He seemed to sag, slightly. "Running off, I don't know about that."

Again, he looked up at the house. His wife still sat on the porch. He gave her another gentle wave. She didn't move.

It was time for me to go. "You'll need to keep an eye out for Rolla," I said.

"He's a coward," Merle said.

"True. But he's also a psychopath. He'll do what he wants. If he comes after you, it'll be from behind, in the dark."

"Yeah," he said. "But he won't want to mess with Newt."

"I hope not," I said.

I made my way to the Lexus. Laurel Stafford watched me from the porch. She didn't respond to my wave either.

As I drove through the desert back to town, I went over what had happened. Rollo Kohler might have understood that Newt was ready to kill him.

He might want no part of either of the two Marines. But he wasn't finished with me.

I had another thought. One of those involved in this mess had the training and skill to snap a neck. I couldn't quite see why Newt Ragatz would want to kill Gale Dunn or Joe Kohler, but it was hard to tell what might motivate the young man. He hadn't come home yet, and he might not for some time. I knew.

Returned to The World, I had lived my life in the deserts and the dark alleys of the heart. I disguised myself, fled myself, hid myself from myself.

I rarely thought of Nam. Once in a while, an unbeckoned image might appear: a face sweaty and smeared with red dust, a path disappearing into a stand of elephant grass, the odd flopping of helicopter blades, the flare dangling from a parachute and swinging in the night sky. Sometimes a sudden noise might crunch me into a fighting crouch. Otherwise, Nam was finished.

I didn't seek out other vets. I didn't tell war stories. Neither did I attend reunions. I didn't want to see the men I'd served with. I had been closer to them than to anyone in my life except my grandparents and my daughter. But I stayed away.

Then the company decided to hold a reunion on the twentieth anniversary of the fall of Saigon. They decided to hold it in Reno. I could have managed to avoid meeting them, but finally I felt compelled to attend. Semper Fi.

We gathered in the banquet room of Harrah's—beards and ponytails and razor cuts, silk ties and tee-shirts, limps and leans, scars, prosthetics. Some of us were physical or emotional or psychological wrecks. Some of us were, or at least seemed to be, secure in our lives and our selves.

I discovered that I remembered the name and face, however altered, of every man there who had served under me. I knew as well the name and face of every man who wasn't with us. I knew every action that had taken a man, severely wounded or dead, from the platoon.

I was overwhelmed by their greeting.

They knew. They had been there, betrayed, abandoned. I was one of them.

And they told me what I'd always known. There was no escape.

Some weeks after they left, I took an impromptu trip to Washington and The Wall. I broke down.

Newt hadn't. Yet.

SIXTEEN

Frank was still comatose. That the doctors declared this a positive development did not console his sister. She could read the electronic measurements of his erratic heartbeat and blood pressure, hear the congestion in his lungs, see his discomfort on his gray face.

I tried unsuccessfully to take her again for coffee. I couldn't get her to talk. She had closed up, shut down.

She was attending Frank, watching with him, as if in some ancient ritual. She'd been unable to sit so with her husband, for Randy had died within minutes of being stricken. Now she would stay and watch and wait.

I left her to her vigil.

At Off Limits, only two cars nosed into slots painted on the tarmac lot. One was the black BMW driven by Snooks Hale, one a new steel-gray Lamborghini. As I parked the Lexus, a white SUV pulled in beside me. Paulie Hauberk got out and waited till I joined him.

I nodded at the Lamborghini. "Pretty racy ride for a septuagenarian."

He shrugged, took out a phone, punched a number, waited, spoke, "Outside. Ross."

After a moment, he slipped the phone back in his pocket, jerking his square head toward the front door, which opened before we reached it. Snooks smiled. "I've got a feeling we're about to have us some fun, Paulie."

The square man nudged me inside. Without the special lighting, the stages and elevated platforms made the big room look like a play area for giant rodents. The smell of chemical cleaners tainted the air. A couple of men in shirtsleeves set up bottles behind the bar. A couple of women in hot pants and halters drifted among tables as if lost.

In one of the booths Len Maglie sat dressed for yachting, bright brassy buttons on his blue blazer. He shot cuffs linked by twists of gold. Snooks slid in beside him.

"I suppose you're wondering why I called this meeting," I said.

Maglie grumbled a laugh. "To give me my money. Better be."

"Sorry," I said. "All I have to give you is my resignation."

He didn't laugh at that. His rumbling voice deepened. "I don't think so."

"Then think again. I'm done looking for Howie Ragatz. It's all bullshit."

He did his hand trick, raised it, made it a fist, turned it one way, then the other. If it was supposed to intimidate me, it succeeded. "You think so, huh?"

"I think you've been lying to me from the get-go. I think you set up the robbery of Bryce Ragatz. You knew about his deal with Harvey Prior. You knew when and where the money would be. You figured a plan, suckered in Howie. He took on Dick Pym and Joe Kohler, they jumped Ragatz and Paulie here, who got his hand blown off, and Pym got killed, and Joe got jailed, and Howie got the money, which you took after you killed him."

Beside me, Paulie Hauberk's breathing changed.

"Is he saying I got your hand shot off, Paulie?" A grin rearranged the lumps of his face. "He thinks I'm a bad man?"

"He thinks you're a septuagenarian," Paulie said, stone-faced.

"Whatever the fuck that is." Len Maglie unclenched his fist as he looked at me with what appeared to be genuine, even amused interest. "So why would I have you look for him then, if I killed him?"

"Cover," I said. "To make it look like you didn't know what actually went down. And to keep tabs on me, what I learned."

"And what was that?"

"Bits and pieces," I said. "For instance, I learned that a while back, Gale Dunn started making late night, drunken phone calls. I'm guessing that if she'd called anybody about Howie, she'd call you. And everybody she talked to she accused, so she would have babbled about how she knew you were in on the robbery with Howie, how she thought you probably killed him. You couldn't have that kind of talk out there. You had her shut up."

"She fell off a fucking tractor, I heard." He still seemed interested, entertained.

"I don't think so," I said. "Her neck was broken, like Joe Kohler's."

He smiled then. "You think I killed, what, three people in this deal? Howie Ragatz and Gale Dunn and Joe fucking Kohler?"

"That's what I think, yeah." It was a mish-mash of hunch, guess, and speculation. But if it wasn't the truth, it had truth in it. "The money really was yours, after Howie stole it from Bryce Ragatz and you stole it from Howie. You probably spent it on your fancy duds."

"Duds, huh?" His hand was again a fist, up, turning. But he wasn't angry. He was enjoying this. "I got money enough to buy duds. Why would I want to steal two hundred and fifty thousand dollars of Bryce Ragatz's money? Besides the fact that it's a lot of green."

Disconnected thoughts had been floating around in my mind. Now they came together to form a question. "The story was that when all this was going on, you managed to persuade your father-in-law it was time he retired. How exactly did you do that?"

His hand stopped turning. He hadn't liked the question.

I went on, guessing some more. "Whoever stole the money Prior paid Bryce Ragatz was messing with Prior's business. Showing him he'd lost control. Guys he depended on, the way you depend on Snooks here, and Paulie, would see that the old man couldn't hack it anymore. That it was time for Harvey to go. Make it a lot easier for you to take over."

He shrugged pleasantly. "But that doesn't explain why I'd want to kill Howie Ragatz."

And suddenly I found myself slipped into a different mode. In Nam we talked about a negative give-a-fuck factor. Mine was high.

"I don't know, Maglie. But he knew you were involved in the robbery, and he always needed money, he could maybe want it from you, maybe hold the robbery over your head, try to use it against you. Besides, why split it? You probably planned to kill him all along."

"Yeah, I'm a killer all right," he said, grinning now. "What are you planning to do about all this?"

"Nothing," I said. "I can't prove any of it. Nobody much cares anyhow. There's a young nurse who'd like to know who her father is, but otherwise . . ."

"No cops?"

I shrugged.

He smiled then. "That's too bad. It could have been fun." He slid out of the booth, stood, and removed his jacket. He undid his belt, let his trousers slip, and tugged down on his shorts, exposing the sag of his old man's abdomen, the hang of his old man's genitals.

"One look at this, Ross, and the cops would crack up when you told them that tale."

The appendectomy scar was old, on the white skin a fine, whiter line.

"The night of the robbery, and after, I was in no shape to do anything to anybody. The hospital has records."

The scar on his abdomen, the rumble of amusement in his voice, the grin on his lumpy ugly face all argued that he was telling me the truth. Len Maglie hadn't killed Howie Ragatz.

But that didn't mean the rest of it wasn't true. Or close to it.

"Maybe," I said, "But I keep telling people, I don't really care what happened to Howie Ragatz. And right now, I've got more important things to worry about. A friend of mine is in the ICU at Renown, and I'm off to sit with him. That's important. Not Howie Ragatz. Not you."

I thought then I'd gone too far. He pulled up his shorts and trousers, stuffed down his shirt, zipped up, fixed his belt, all while his face darkened with blood. He stood before me, rocking on the balls of his feet, both hands now fists, face ugly, eyes hard. Beside me, Paulie took a deep breath.

"Too much trouble, Len." This from Snooks, as he slid out of the booth. "It'll complicate things."

Len Maglie continued to rock. "I can handle it."

"Probably." Snooks shrugged.

"Probably?" Len Maglie looked at him as if seeing for the first time what had always been there.

And he slowly stopped rocking. He picked up his blazer and slipped into it as the color faded from his face. "Get him the fuck out of here."

Snooks gave me a nod. I stepped back and turned toward the door. Then Maglie spoke again. "About that little girl's daddy. All you need to do is look at her."

I stopped, turned back. "I have."

"Then, you dumb fuck, look at me."

As soon as he said it, I saw it. Not his face, features. His squat body, his wedge-like torso, wide, powerful. And my heart sank.

He laughed at me. "She was another bit of business Harvey couldn't control. Got roughed up a little. Knocked up a little."

If I'd had a gun, I'd have shot him.

Snooks Hale followed me to the door and, as before, out it. "You owe me, Ross."

The afternoon was ebbing. A few flat white clouds tried to make the sky interesting. The city hissed. I was tired, hungry, irritable.

"I don't think so," I said. "I'd say we were pretty much even, since I just gave you what you wanted."

"The robbery stuff, yeah," he said easily. "So how much of that is true?"

"Enough," I said. "The cops have been looking into it lately. An anonymous call to RPD would get him tangled up. He'd be distracted. And he'd look disloyal. He might find himself in the position he put Harvey Prior in years ago."

Snooks grinned. "You're old, Ross, and you're crazy, but you aren't stupid."

"Neither is Len Maglie," I said.

He stopped smiling. "I can handle Len."

"Have fun."

It was too late for lunch, too early for dinner. I got a drive-through hot dog to sustain me as I pushed on now to end things. That meant another visit to the neighborhood of big trees and old homes and notions of another time.

Bryce Ragatz answered the door.

"You're off the hook," I said.

He didn't ask for an explanation. He invited me in, showed me into the same room his wife and I had used. He offered me a drink, which I turned down. Out on the lawn among the rose bushes, there was no sign of the lost, lonesome quail.

I said, sitting. "DNA says you're not the father of Gale Dunn's daughter."

"I didn't notice till the next day that the sweatband was gone," he said. As he sat, the late afternoon light slicked his scar. "I've been expecting to hear from you."

"Now that you know he's innocent," Carlotta Farragut Ragatz said, entering. She took up a position at her husband's shoulder, as if to guard him. "You can leave us alone."

"He's not Mia Dunn's father," I said. "As for his innocence, that's another matter."

Bryce Ragatz folded his hands serenely. "You always were a moralist, Jack. Good and bad. Guilt. Blame. That's probably why you've been discontented most of your life."

"Two people are dead," I said. "An angry drunken woman and a vicious old thug. They aren't widely lamented, but I'd like to know why they were killed."

"Killed?" Carlotta Farragut Ragatz stiffened. "Now you're trying to involve us in—in what? Murder? Is that what you're saying?"

"No," I said. "I'm saying that the set of circumstances that led to these two deaths was begun by a bored war hero who wanted to have a little fun flying drugs into town from Mexico."

Bryce Ragatz smiled his warm, charming smile.

"That's what it was, wasn't it?" I was having trouble controlling my anger. "Fun. A game. You against all the authorities with all their fancy equipment, radar and all that. The excitement. Even riskier than cuckolding Reno husbands. I imagine the money didn't matter that much."

"It helped," he said easily, "but you're right. It wasn't the reason."

"Bryce," his wife cautioned, "Don't talk about this to him. He's a . . . a . . ."

"A lawyer," said Bryce Ragatz. "He knows the law has nothing to say about anything I might have done all those years ago."

She wasn't satisfied. "He's little better than a thug himself, like his grandfather. He'll want something, he'll try to use it to . . ."

"Let it go, Lottie," her husband said quietly. She turned to stare angrily out the window.

"What I don't get," I said, "is why you were taking the money into the casino. Were you washing it?"

He smiled again. "It became table-games income. I even paid taxes on it. It made the numbers look a little better, got me a better price when I sold out, maybe. But again, finally, it wasn't that important."

"Why'd you stop?"

Behind him, his wife stood stiffly, her shoulders beginning to shudder.

He shrugged. "Harvey was almost a friend, basically harmless. Maglie, though, is a vicious bastard. I told him I was done. He wasn't happy, but he couldn't do much about it."

"Except kill you," I said.

He smiled. "Another risk to take. But not much of one."

"What about the money?" Carlotta Farragut Ragatz turned suddenly. "The money Randy Barnes stole?"

"It paid for the education of a nurse," I said. "Think of it as an investment."

"Stolen money." She'd managed to work herself into a fury. "All the time parading around like he was the nicest, kindest, most sincere man in town and he was hopping in bed with a whore, stealing my husband's money, he was nothing but an embezzler, a common thief, the way his wife was a just another adulteress."

I looked out the window. Grass going dormant. Rose bushes. Not a bird in sight.

I wanted to be in the desert.

SEVENTEEN

Frank was conscious but dopey, drifting in and out of sleep. Awake, he spoke little and weakly. He seemed surprised to be alive.

Alicia, haggard, greeted me with a feeble smile. We sat together, listening to Frank breathe, listening as well to the hospital hiss and hum. Soon Frank's middle son and wife arrived and pressed Alicia to go home, or at least to dinner. I joined the effort, offering to take her to a decent seafood restaurant a few blocks away, and finally she assented. After a long time in the ladies' room, she emerged looking less drawn, more vital. In half an hour we were seated at a quiet table in the candle-lit Wells Avenue establishment, enjoying Chablis and our meals.

We had little to say. Wary, we were hesitant to speak for fear of fanning cooling ashes back into flame. But eventually the soft flickering light from candles in glass globes, as well as the food and wine, put Alicia at ease. She began to speak—of her brother, his condition and her fears; of our daughter, whom she had phoned; of her still tentative plans to sell her house and to travel, perhaps with our granddaughter.

"I won't go alone," she said. "It's awkward, being single. The world isn't set up to accommodate just one. You must have noticed that."

I spooned my lobster bisque. "Yes."

"You never remarried." She had remarked on this a couple of days before but seemed to have forgotten. I thought how, not too long ago, such a comment would have been an oblique accusation, a hint at some sort of inadequacy. Now it seemed an obscure, unconscious eruption.

"I circled around it a couple of times," I said. "But I do better alone, I guess."

"No wonder, the way you were raised . . ." She looked at me, fell silent for a moment, then went on. "Frank was right, wasn't he? You married me to become part of our family."

I knew to be careful here. "Maybe. Partly. But I was in love with you."

"In lust, more like." Shadows cast by the wavering candle flame played on her features, hollowed her cheeks, sculpted the bone beneath the flesh. "But you were in effect an orphan. What you really wanted was to be part of a real family."

"I was. My grandparents loved me," I began loyally. "They—"

"They were old, and tired, and still guilty about failing your mother."

That was true. It wasn't the whole truth, though. But I let it go.

"And you wanted to be part of a family that wouldn't have you."

I was uncertain now. "Your parents were always decent to me, Alicia, at least before we split. They never made me feel awkward or unwelcome."

She leaned back, as if to view me from a new perspective. "They argued against our marriage until the day we said I do, Jack."

"They weren't enthusiastic, I knew that," I said. "But that was because I wasn't Italian or Catholic. But I liked them. I thought I could change their minds, bring them around."

"You were Frank's friend." Reflected yellow candle flames danced in her dark eyes. "That was enough to get you a place at the dinner table once in a while. That was all."

Around us, voices murmured, as if confessing secrets.

"You weren't what they wanted for me. They wanted an Italian, yes, and a Catholic, maybe even somebody to take over Dad's plumbing business, once it became clear that Frank wasn't interested. They wanted me to find a man who would give me a safe, secure little life like theirs. A respectable man, which for all your efforts you weren't."

She was right. I'd been a high school athlete, which earned me a certain legitimacy, as had my graduation from UNR, my USMC commission, and my matriculation in Stanford Law. But for many, all this was only a veneer of propriety covering a reality dark, seedy, even sordid. My father was unknown, his identity a subject of speculation and crude humor. My mother was believed to have been at best a loose woman killed in a bar fight in Tonopah. I'd grown up on the streets and in a cramped apartment over a bail-bond business, within siren distance of the police station. My grandmother was peculiar. My grandfather was thought a shady character in a sleazy business, and I often helped him with it. I was not respectable.

I tested a small, self-deprecating smile. "*The Creature from the Black Lagoon*."

Alicia ignored that, as she should. Old movie. Bad joke.

"They didn't dislike you personally, I mean," she said. "At least not until you ran out on me and Cyndi."

That wasn't quite right. When I left, I hadn't known Alicia was pregnant. But now I said nothing, fit my spoon into my splinted hand, ate.

"Except," Alicia continued, "'ran out' isn't the correct phrase, is it?"

"Close enough," I said.

Her eyebrow edged up expectantly.

I hesitated. I didn't want a repeat of the scene in Emile's. But I had something to say.

"I've tried to live honorably," I began, "if I can use that old-fashioned word. I've tried to be honest and trustworthy."

But the words sounded affected, even to me. They didn't say what I meant. I tried it from the other end.

"I came back from Nam angry, and crazy, and I got into all that 'nasty notoriety' stuff Carlotta Farragut Ragatz mentioned. I killed a couple of men that I might not actually have had to, I mistreated others, I made a couple of women unhappy. I picked fights with you. I regret all that. But I regret most what I did before I went to war."

Even now I hadn't come to terms with it, a minor matter to many people, but after fifty years still gnawing, rat-like, at my conscience. I'd broken a promise. I'd violated a trust. I'd dishonored myself.

We'd married when I graduated from UNR. Fifteen months later we were in Palo Alto. I studied law. Alicia worked in the university Architecture Office. I'd joined the Marine Corps Reserve in college, trained summers, and enrolled in a program that would assign me, finished with law school, duties on a command staff or perhaps a billet with JAG. I would gain excellent experience, make contacts helpful once I was back in civilian life. We would return to Reno, I would join one of the better firms, while Alicia would do what the wives of young professionals did—entertain, work on civic and charitable campaigns, support causes. We would have a child or two and a home in an upscale neighborhood and friends among the politically and culturally active. We would be happy.

In the sexual stupor of our courtship, I had promised Alicia all that, because that was what she said she wanted and she was what I wanted. Then, without discussing it with her, in a move as craven as it was disloyal, I volunteered for active duty.

Now Alicia watched me. Something in her expression compelled caution.

"I didn't want the life you'd planned, that I'd agreed to. It had come to seem unreal. I came to feel that way about myself too."

I'd had no idea what I really wanted, but it wasn't to spend my life filing briefs and preparing contracts and arguing legalities. I didn't want croquet and cocktail parties and dress-up dinners.

"I loved you," I said, "but I'd made a terrible mistake, marrying you."

Alicia's expression, in the candlelight, twisted through a sequence of contortions, settling finally on a sneer. "Terrible."

I shrugged. It was complicated. I wasn't sure that even now I could sort it out.

The young woman I thought I'd married had never existed. I'd made her up, a figure out of my deepest longing, but Alicia had turned out to be a real, actual person, one I was unprepared to deal with. I found her, ultimately, disappointing, insubstantial. She found me, finally, irritating and pretentious. We found each other difficult, then impossible to talk with.

There had been nights, many, when as Alicia slept I sat at our kitchen table, trying to study, and dejection like a thick, gray ooze weighted down my arms and shoulders so that I could barely lift my hand to turn a textbook page. Depression seeped into my skull, numbing, dulling. I couldn't think. Nothing seemed real to me.

I tried again. "I had all kinds of reasons for opting for combat. A Marine's a warrior, and I couldn't let other Marines die when I did nothing, and my country needed me, blah blah. I managed to convince myself of all this, and I got angry when you didn't accept it. And my anger somehow justified my decision."

Alicia had grown very still, seemed barely to breathe.

"True or not, though, it was an exercise in self-deception. I didn't realize till much later that none of the reasons I'd concocted was really to the point."

Her mouth moved slightly, stiffly. The candle in the glass orb between us flickered wildly, threatening to gutter. "Which was?"

"That I couldn't give you what you wanted. That I'd never be able to make you happy."

She sat stiffly, still. "Why didn't you just say so?"

I sighed. I was guilty. Why bother to explain? But I tried to.

"I didn't know it then. It took me a long time, long after I got back from Nam, to see that I'd married you to escape being alone but now I was more alone than ever. Then I made things worse. Like a coward, I ran, I betrayed everything I thought I valued, all I thought I was."

I hadn't quite got it right.

"I'd made promises. Vows. I couldn't bring myself to break them, to end things. So I persuaded myself that going off to war was my duty. It put the problem somewhere in the future. It gave me breathing room.

Maybe I'd change my mind. Maybe I'd see an honorable way out. Maybe I'd die."

Alicia was listening, carefully, but not sympathetically.

"I thought I was a man of his word." I looked at her. "When I volunteered for combat, I demonstrated that my word was worth nothing."

Even after all these years, even just thinking about it, I felt the heat rise up my neck, the clot of shame collect in my throat.

Alicia too had colored. "Do you hear how silly you sound, Jack? From a grown man? Almost fifty years after the fact?"

I did. Now. Saying it.

"And you're doing it again, damn you! The same thing you did then."

Before I could speak, she went on. "It's all you, you, you—like I wasn't part of it, like I was helpless, a victim."

That was true. I had thought of her so. Even though I knew better.

She leaned forward, into the shadowing candlelight. "But I was way ahead of you. Long before you left, even before we married, if you want the truth, I could see it probably wasn't going to work."

She seemed to enjoy the effect that had on me.

"My God, Jack—don't you remember: the spats, the mix-ups, the silences? We were always failing each other, always making up. Once we were married, alone with each other, stuck with each other, everything intensified."

She spoke now with an excited, almost triumphant energy. "Our marriage was a huge mistake. But it was *our* marriage, *our* mistake, not just yours."

She glared at me, commanding agreement. "And if we didn't share anything, if we couldn't talk, if we didn't even much like each other, if something had to be done about it, *we* had to do it, *us*, the two of us, Jack."

I knew what was coming.

"Then you did it alone. I had no say in it. I didn't matter."

She was right, of course. "Yes."

She tossed her napkin down onto her plate in disgust. The flame of the table candle again flickered in its glass. "Even now, all you're concerned with is your stupid honor, your integrity."

"Yes."

But something was not quite right. It didn't seem enough, now, my deciding on my own to leave, not enough to fuel her fifty years of hostility.

"Then, rightly," I said, "you dumped me, told me in the same letter that you were filing for divorce and that I was going to be a father."

"You'd left, went off to play war," she said. "And made all your promises lies. And I was bitter. You became who you really were, and I felt used, tricked, betrayed."

"Yes, but—"

"Besides," she said, "you were so wrapped up in yourself, in notions of manhood and all that macho crap, you never saw that I was already gone."

That stopped me. "What?"

Her smile brightened with angry pleasure. "I had Randy waiting for me."

Randy Barnes and I were taking classes together. He was at our apartment regularly. I sometimes caught him watching Alicia, shyly, yearning.

"I knew he had a crush on you," I said slowly. "I wasn't surprised you married him as soon as our divorce was final. But I never imagined that you and he would get together."

"Don't imagine it now," she snapped.

I watched her.

Then, more calmly, she said, "I didn't even know, really, consciously, that I was encouraging him, getting him ready . . . except down deep, I suppose I must have. I felt it. But I didn't sleep with Randy until we were married."

Although it could not possibly matter, I was glad to hear that.

"And I didn't sleep with anyone else, ever, after I married him."

Why she added that I didn't know. Nor did I know why it too made me glad.

Alicia said then, still quietly, "Those last couple of months, living with you, smiling at Randy, I've never felt so guilty. But I didn't know why, I couldn't say, even to myself . . . So I got angry. Then when you left, it was easier to be angry than to try to understand why I felt the way I did. It stayed easy, all these years."

Guilt and anger. She had reduced decades of animosity to their essence.

"You ran off to war. You'd rather face dying than me. Was I that frightening, Jack?"

I hadn't been afraid of facing Alicia. I'd been afraid of facing myself.

"I'm still angry with you. You lied. You betrayed me," she said. "But I betrayed you too."

I wasn't sure what that meant, but now, after all those years, finally it didn't matter.

"And we both failed our daughter."

I wasn't sure I understood this, either. Our daughter had often been at the center of our nastier arguments. I'd missed her birth and infancy, and I felt guilty about it. Alicia knew that, kept throwing it in my face. She accused me of failing to participate actively and wholly in Cynthia's upbringing; I pleaded the uncertainties of my work. I argued that Alicia spent more time with her social-climbing friends and their do-gooding than she did with Cynthia; she insisted that I was merely projecting my own inadequacies. We tried not to involve our child in our disputes, not to let her see us being unpleasant to one another, but we had not always succeeded.

Alicia saw my uncertainty. "Why do you think she waited so long to marry? She was in her mid-thirties."

"If you mean we didn't set a very good example for her," I said, "I agree there."

"There are probably a lot of things we could agree on, now," she said.

No doubt. I took a swallow of wine. "If we'd talked like this all those years ago, could we have avoided the strife?"

"Probably not," she said. "It wouldn't have changed us. We are what we are."

I nodded.

She looked at me then, gave me a small smile, as if in recognition. "Besides, we couldn't have had this conversation before, Jack. We weren't old. We hadn't come to the dying time."

We had lived long lives, she meant, and now could see the end. Concerns shriveled. Dross fell away. Mortality made things clear, if we cared to see.

But for now we'd had enough, Alicia and I, of the meal, of each other. I called for the bill. Soon we were out in the night.

I'd just started the Lexus when Alicia asked, "Are you going to find out who the young nurse's father is, Jack?

"No," I said. "There's no way now to be sure."

I hadn't realized that I'd decided to tell that to Mia Dunn. I certainly didn't want to tell her that her father was a vicious ugly thug who had raped her mother. I had only the rapist's word on that, which wasn't enough. Even if I knew it was probably the truth.

"And Randy?"

"You knew him," I said. "You know what kind of man he was. That really should tell you everything you need to know."

"He was a good man," she said quietly.

He'd stolen money. He'd lusted, at least in his heart. Even so . . .

I remembered then what Carlotta Farragut Ragatz had said only a few hours before. That Alicia was an adulteress. The implication was, certainly, that she had slept with Bryce Ragatz. But Alicia had told me that she had been faithful to Randy Barnes. Which meant . . .

I nearly spoke, then thought better of it. It didn't matter. I put the Lexus into drive and steered it toward the street.

Alicia's car was in the Renown parking garage, but she wanted to go up and say goodnight to Frank. I decided to let her do it alone.

But before she got out, I asked, "Not that it matters, but if you thought all along that it probably wasn't going to work, why did you marry me?"

She looked out at the traffic on Mill Street, beyond it to the lights and life of Reno.

"Maybe," she began, "maybe because I was like the dancer, like Gale Dunn. And like your mother. I wanted more. And you were the only chance I'd ever have to get it."

HOME, I SHOWERED. Manipulating my hand to avoid getting the wrap of the splint wet was an irksome chore. I dried off, got into a robe, and found a pair of sharp scissors.

The ER doctors had said I'd need the splint for from three to six weeks, but it looked and felt ratty, and I was tired of it. I cut it off. My hand wasn't swollen or discolored, and when I carefully clenched my fingers I felt no pain. I tossed the splint into the garbage.

The act seemed almost symbolic. I was finished doing what I didn't do anymore.

I'd tried. I'd just told Alicia all that I could tell her. Tomorrow I would give Mia Dunn the bad news, saving her from news immeasurably worse. If she still wasn't satisfied, if she still wanted to track down her father, I'd recommend a couple of good agencies. But if she had to learn that her father was a psychopathic goon, and that when her mother looked at Mia she had, almost certainly, seen the man who had raped her, she wasn't going to learn it from me.

In bed I went back over the dinner conversation with Alicia. We had advanced. We would never be anything but exes, but we might be able to relax in the other's presence. Maybe.

The next morning, I was again high above McCarran Boulevard as dawn became day. Frost grayed the sagebrush. In the still, cold air, a thin spread of smoke hovered over the Sierra foothills. On the streets, traffic went its early-morning way. I worked up a decent sweat, felt little pain, jogged almost happily along.

Back at the house, I showered and dressed, then turned on the television news as I fixed a green pepper scramble. The school district was being sued by parents of special students. The mayor announced that she would encourage the city council to commission more sculpture for downtown. Sparks police were looking for witnesses to a road-rage incident near Reed

High School. A fire in the early hours of the morning had destroyed a home in Caughlin Ranch.

The screen filled with firemen and trucks and hoses. Behind them stood a broken section of a native, rust-colored rock wall. Collapsed planks and beams smoldered, a caved-in deck yawned, and wide glassless windows gaped. Fire had taken half the house. Smoke and water had ruined the rest. The fire marshal suspected arson.

Reportedly, a single occupant had been home at the time of the blaze. Authorities had not yet given out a name or condition.

I stood, numb, suspended. I couldn't think or feel. I couldn't connect.

The screen changed. The newsreader babbled. The screen changed again. Again.

I was still standing there when my phone rang. It was my daughter.

"Dad?"

The voice didn't sound like Cynthia's. It was the voice of a child.

"Dad?"

It came this time as a soft, beseeching wail. She couldn't say what I didn't want to hear.

EIGHTEEN

The fire had started—had been set—outside the utility room beside the garage. The fire marshal discovered that two lines of the automatic sprinkler system, which hadn't been checked for some time, had failed to function properly. The flames spread rapidly, giving off noxious fumes. Awakened by the smoke alarm, Alicia had managed to crawl out to the stairway before the smoke overcame and then killed her.

She hadn't been burned, so there was no question of identity. Still, a relative or close friend had to make the identification official. Authorities had found Cynthia's address and phone number among Alicia's papers. They called Seattle.

Cynthia had referred them to me.

She was flying down. Her plane was scheduled to arrive in midafternoon. I would pick her up. She would stay with me for two nights, until her husband was able to get here, at which time they would check into a hotel.

Once able to speak, she had given me all this in the paint-by-numbers mode of the deeply shocked.

"I'll see you soon, honey," I said.

For a moment she didn't reply. Then, her voice softer, her suffering less constrained, she said, "Mom called me last night. She said the two of you went to dinner. You talked."

"Yes," I said.

"Yes," she repeated. "I'm glad."

I had no appetite, but I forced myself to eat some of the meal I'd made. I drank coffee. I waited for a phone call.

I was angry. Anger overrides guilt.

Rollo Kohler hadn't been out to kill Alicia, I guessed, but he wouldn't much care that he had. He set fire to her house to get back at me. Because I had humiliated him. Because I couldn't just be what I'd become, an old man living out his boring life.

And I was resolved.

Since I had agreed to look into the matter of Mia Dunn's letter, I'd done things I knew were wrong. Minor things, of little moment, but still wrong. Against the law. Now I was about to do something more serious. I didn't know exactly what, but I knew I was going to do it.

My phone rang.

An hour later, I stepped into the chilly scrubbed space of the Washoe County morgue. A deputy forensic pathologist and an RPD detective met me. Soon we three stood over the body.

She looked younger in death than she had in life. Her skin was pale and soft. Her eyelids were naturally darkened. I had kissed those eyelids, years ago, when we were other people in another world. The soft droop of her lower lip hinted at a pout. I had often been puzzled, sometimes pleased by that pout. Over the years I had found it convenient to forget how deeply Alicia could please me.

Now she was dead. I was at least partly responsible. I would have to live with my part in her death until I too died.

I nodded. Alicia Calvetti Barnes.

The forensic pathologist told me that she would perform the autopsy required for deaths deemed suspicious. The detective asked me if I knew anyone who might have had a grievance against Alicia Barnes. Against Alicia? No. I told him about our dinner the previous evening and whom he could speak to regarding her movements after that. He made a couple of notes and said he might want to talk to me again.

I walked out of the chill into the cold.

For a moment I stood on the sidewalk. Renown Medical Center was just down the street. I could stop and see Frank, who no doubt had been told of his sister's death. But I wasn't ready to face him. Not yet. I had something else to do.

I drove home. In my office I opened the locked drawer of my desk. Certificates, titles, policies. The Ragatz files. Photographs. The teak box. My grandfather's .38 Smith and Wesson.

I put the gun in my coat pocket and I locked up my house and I left.

Driving to Sparks, I checked occasionally for a tail, but I really didn't care if I was being followed. I really didn't care about anything.

I'd been in this mood, this condition, this psychological space, before. I'd been a little crazy then. I was a little crazy now.

The red pickup was parked at the curb. I pulled to a stop behind it, got out, and took the .38 from my pocket. It felt good in my hand, weighty. Significant.

The pickup suggested Rollo Kohler's presence, but the house had about it an aura of emptiness. Roof shingles seemed shoddier. Drapes sagged across the windows. Pigeon poop smeared the entry ramp. The lawn was still soggy.

Pressing the pistol to my thigh, I made my way to the front door. My knock seemed to echo inside. I knocked again. Nothing.

The lock offered little challenge. The knob turned under my hand. The door swung easily open into a living room empty but for a ratty couch and a television set. The shag carpet was tracked with grease and oil and recent mud.

Inside, I stopped, listened. Still nothing. The house was cold.

As certain as sense and intuition would allow that no one was present, I still cautiously made my way through the rest of the house. Two bedrooms, in the larger the bed stripped, bureau drawers and closet yawning, in the other a queen with greasy sheets and a huge television screen and porno DVDs and a step-climbing machine and a set of free weights. The bathroom was gray with grime. Kitchen appliances were crusted with cooking slops and the floor was sticky. The tap dripped into a stained sink.

Both the glass and screen doors to the deck stood open. Just beyond them, on the wooden flooring grooved by the roll of Joe Kohler's wheelchair, blood coagulated in a shiny, paint-like pool. Stepping forward, I saw the flow of gore that narrowed back to its source.

Rollo Kohler was dead. His beautiful blue eyes were open, dried out. Much of the rest of his face was gone.

Someone with a large caliber gun had shot him in the back of the head. The bullet, exiting, had blasted away bone and bearded flesh, teeth, cheek, chin.

What it meant most to me was that I was too late. Not quite rational, silent, still, I raged. I'd been cheated of my chance to do what I didn't do anymore.

"Fun."

I didn't bother to turn around. Paulie Hauberk moved up beside me. The pistol in his hand was so big he seemed, with his other hand a black rubber absence, unbalanced, atilt. His gun too was a Smith and Wesson, what looked like a .460 Magnum.

"This you?"

"No," I said. "You?"

He didn't bother to reply. Instead, he asked, "When?"

I guessed. "Early this morning, from the look of the blood."

"Why?"

I shook my head. I didn't know. For sure.

I should have been grateful. Whoever had killed Rollo Koehler had kept me from murder. But I wasn't. I had no vent for my anger, despair, grief.

"So?"

I understood the question. "I'm not here."

I should report the death. But Cynthia would be arriving soon. And I had business to attend to. Another small law broken.

"He'll rot."

"Let him," I said.

"The fire? Your ex?"

I nodded grimly. "She didn't get out."

He was silent. Then he said, "Yeah."

"Yeah," I repeated as a question slipped into my mind. "Why are you here? You still tailing me?"

Again he was silent, now significantly, before he spoke. "Cops this morning. That old robbery. He wants to see you."

"Maglie thinks I fingered him?"

He shrugged.

"I didn't," I said.

He shrugged again.

Slowly I held up my pistol. He watched carefully as I slipped it into my pocket. "I don't have time to fool with Maglie. You'll just have to shoot me."

His mouth made a small smile.

"Except that wouldn't help Maglie, would it?"

His smile slipped away.

"You're a literary man, Paulie. You know what *cui bono* means?"

"You're fucking crazy?"

I laughed. "To whose benefit. Tell Maglie to ask that question. Who benefits from his getting tangled up with the cops? Who would think the time was right for an ambitious fellow to make his move?"

He thought about it. I considered coaxing but decided against it. He'd do what he'd do.

What he did was edge back his coat lapel and slip his pistol into a shoulder holster, put himself back in balance. "Tabby says you're okay. Respectful."

I nodded. "A guy learns how to treat a woman right, reading Max Brand."

As the escalator descended, she stood quietly, her gaze sweeping the airport atrium. She wore comfortable slacks and jacket, sensible shoes. Her face was free of make-up, her brown hair was shorn short and flecked with gray. She was just a middle-aged woman, slim, fit, of the no-nonsense, carefully contained sort. Then her eyes found mine, and she became Cynthia.

She sagged into my embrace. "Dad."

Deplaned passengers stepped around us. A slot machine chimed above the mingle of voices. We held each other.

My daughter finally stepped back. She looked a little like Alicia, nothing like me. Now, her features puffed and twisted by grief, she seemed a crude caricature of herself.

"Did you see her?"

I nodded. As we started slowly off toward the baggage claim, I told her what I most urgently had to: her mother hadn't burned, hadn't felt flames.

While we waited for her luggage, we linked arms. Touching. Comfort of the flesh.

After retrieving her bags and stowing them in the Lexus, I drove home. Cynthia was silent. She hadn't asked me how her mother came to be dead. I wasn't eager to tell her. I didn't know if she would hold me responsible. I did know that I would always hold myself so.

She settled herself in the guest room and then got in the shower. I took my grandfather's pistol from my pocket. I looked at it. It was a fine old weapon. Chet Stander had never used it in any but honorable efforts. The same could not be said of his grandson.

I took the pistol into my office and put it back in its box and locked the desk drawer. Then I called the Sparks Police Department, told the desk sergeant where to send a team and what they'd find. I also told him who I was and that I'd come in the first thing the next morning.

I made coffee. I'd thought Cynthia and I might talk a while, go eat something, then during evening visiting hours stop in to see Frank.

Cynthia came out, fresh-faced, damp-haired, in a maroon University of Washington jogging suit. She looked younger. I felt older.

"I guess you better tell me," she said, sitting.

As I tried to think how to begin, my phone rang. The Sparks Police Department.

Officers would be at my home in ten minutes. I was to remain there until they arrived. If I didn't, a warrant would be sought for my arrest.

I passed the information on to my daughter. Dismay distorted her features. “It was another one of your . . . cases?”

“I was doing a favor for your mother,” I said.

NINETEEN

They kept me until midnight. I volunteered all the information I had, everything I knew for certain. I wrote out and signed a statement. Then I insisted that they charge me or let me go. My grieving daughter needed what comfort I might be able to provide.

I took a cab home. The Lexus was parked under my mulberry tree. A light in the living room was on. As I came in, Cynthia raised up from the couch, her expression an inquiry.

"They're through with me, at least for now," I said. "I told them everything I had to tell."

She stood. "Now you can tell me."

"It's late, kid," I said. "You must be whipped. Why not wait until morning?"

"I can't sleep," she said. "I'll fix some tea."

While she was in the kitchen, I went once again into my office, once again opened the locked lower drawer of my desk. This time I took out the Ragatz files.

In my living room, I spread out on a coffee table what I had to show my daughter: the note from Mia Dunn, the letters from the bank, the photographs, the reports on the disappearance of Howie Ragatz, reports on the robbery of Bryce Ragatz, the autopsy report on Gale Dunn, the documents from the DNA lab. Then, as we drank tea, I told her what all of it meant.

It took a while, but not as long as it had with SPD. Cynthia listened, as she always did, carefully. She was a marine biologist, a gatherer of data, a tester of hypotheses. But her reaction, when I finished, was intuitive: she went straight to the only, for her, important question. "How could mom think that Randy had been unfaithful to her? That's just . . . absurd."

Randy Barnes had been her stepfather. She'd grown up with him. She loved him.

He had been smitten by Gale Dunn, it seemed. He had stolen money from Bryce Ragatz for her. But she had simply toyed with him. So, perhaps because he was an honorable man, perhaps because she was a vixen, he had not violated his wedding vow. He had been faithful. Or so I chose to believe.

"He died," I said, "Alicia was alone, after all those years. When she got the letter, she must have felt . . ." I saw where I was headed, gave it up. Who was I to speak to my daughter of her dead mother's guilt?

"I tried to get her to come up more, to stay longer with us," Cynthia said. "But she had all her meetings and things."

I nodded.

Her eyes filled with tears. "I should have tried harder."

"No," I said. "You aren't responsible for her death, Cynthia."

She turned her glistening eyes toward me. "Neither are you, Dad."

We looked at each other, father and daughter, neither of us quite able to accept the verdict of the other.

Five days later. Storm clouds capped the Sierra. In the foothills and the valley below, scattered snowflakes stuttered and swooped on the wind. In Our Lady of the Snows cemetery, next to the stone that marked Randal Barnes's grave, Alicia's casket sat on straps over the darkness that would receive her. The priest intoned old words that vanished into the gray of the day.

The requiem Mass had been sparsely attended. Most of those at the church service I didn't know—a smattering of elderly couples, women of the parish, a few younger friends of Alicia's nephews.

Cynthia, who had composed a simple, elegant obituary for her mother, was discouraged. As I drove her and Curtis, her husband, to the graveyard, she said, as if to herself, "I didn't know she was so alone. All those years, all the meetings and parties and charity work, I thought she had friends, I thought . . ."

I hadn't known that, either. I should have, at least after I'd been to her home, seen all the empty space, heard the quiet.

Now at the gravesite, only family mourned. Alicia's nephews and their wives, Cynthia and Curtis. And me.

I was not especially welcome. Frank's youngest son had decided that I was responsible, finally, for his aunt's death. Or at least somehow involved. I couldn't blame him.

The murder of Rollo Kohler had been widely reported in the media, the connection to Joe Kohler's death made, to Gale Dunn's not. There was no mention of either Howie or Bryce Ragatz, although I had in my statement identified both. Apparently, Carlotta Farragut Ragatz still had pull. My name, on the other hand, was used in a fashion ambiguous enough to lend credence to any number of speculations.

None of Frank's family said anything, of course, in deference to Cynthia's feelings. She was often at my side, touching me, leaning on me, including me. But alone, I was avoided, subjected to resentful glances, treated as if I were some ghoulish interloper.

I wasn't inclined to try to explain. I'd already done that, to Frank.

To everyone's surprise, he had rallied. He was in pain and dull with drugs but, the doctors said, in no immediate danger. Barring infection, he would heal, could live, properly medicated and monitored, for, well, an indefinite period.

He was not especially happy to hear this.

He was distressed at the death of his sister. He hadn't expected to outlive her. He didn't quite know what to feel.

I hadn't been alone with him until the day before Alicia's funeral. Then, weak and tired, nearly frail, he waved away my proposition that I was responsible for her death. "You, me, Randy, Alicia herself—guilt enough to go around."

When I told him what I thought, he was troubled. "And you haven't gone to the sheriff?"

"No," I said.

"But you're going to?"

"No." I went on, past his protest. "I don't actually *know* anything, Frank. I have no evidence. No proof. It's none of my business, really."

He closed his eyes. "Maybe so, Jack. Maybe so."

And now the snow threatened, the wind whipped, the priest muttered. The casket slid into the hole in the earth. The priest said more words, and it was done.

The family was gathering at the home of Frank's eldest son. I drove Cynthia and Curtis there but didn't go in. I had something else to do.

The heater of the rented Lexus hummed as I drove through the desert. The dirt road, edged with frosty weeds, gave up little dust. I drove slowly, in no hurry to get where I was going.

The sign still read "Stafford Cabinetry." The road still climbed up to the lot. The white, blue-shuttered, improbable house still rose from the desert. But everything was different now.

The Audi was parked under the carport. Beside it, where Merle Stafford's pickup usually stood, was the little blue Toyota. I pulled in behind it.

In the window from which Laurel Stafford had watched me the day I first came out, now another ghostly face loomed. Newt Ragatz. A Marine trained to kill. He saw me looking, lifted two fingers in a mock salute. Then the window was empty.

I got out and started for the house. When I reached the porch, the front door opened. Mia Dunn gave me an anxious smile. "Mr. Ross?"

She saw my face and slipped into silence.

"I'm sorry, Mia," I said. "I did the best I could. But it was so long ago, so many of the people involved are gone or dead."

She wobbled, stumbled to a seat at the white wrought-iron table. The thin cardigan draped over her wide shoulders couldn't have held out the cold, but she appeared not to notice.

"I guess I knew," she said. She took a deep and fortifying breath. "But I had to try."

I sat beside her and told her what I could.

She began to nod long before I finished. "That means it has to be either the man at that club, or else Randal Barnes?"

I didn't want to lie to her. But I didn't want to damage her either.

"Harvey Prior, maybe," I said. "But he was in the business of selling the favors of women. So who knows? What I can say with some assurance is that Randy Barnes was not your father. I knew him. People say that he liked your mother and wanted to help her, but I'm persuaded that he didn't sleep with her. I could be wrong, but I don't think so."

She hugged herself. "You knew him?"

I agreed. "He was a friend." Then I added, "He was married to my ex-wife."

"I suppose Mrs. Barnes is happy," she said bitterly, "now that you can tell her he didn't cheat on her?"

She didn't know. After a moment, I said, "Mrs. Barnes died in a fire a few nights ago."

"Oh! Oh!" The cries came as puffs of emotion. She hugged herself more tightly. Her green eyes threatened tears. "That was her? I'm sorry, so sorry."

I was debating what, if anything, to tell her about the fire when the door opened. Newt Ragatz touched the young woman's shoulder. "Come in. It's cold."

With his small, delicate hands he urged her up. I followed them into the house. Newt nodded toward the living room. "She's gone again."

Mia Dunn lifted her head, straightened her shoulders. "I'll take care of her."

Laurel Stafford sat primly at the edge of the sofa. She wore velvet and tweed, small green earrings, dark high heels. She was lovely. She wasn't there.

Mia sat beside her, took her hand.

"She goes away," Newt said quietly. "Sometimes I envy her."

Mia, plain and squat, watched the beautiful, absent woman, but when she spoke, it was to me. "The fire? Was it part of . . . everything? Everything about me?"

"No," I said without thinking. If that wasn't true, I didn't care. I turned to Newt. "You still have the Glock? Can I see it?"

If he read anything in my request, he didn't show it. "Hang on."

Soon his slightly uneven tread sounded on the stairway to the second floor. Mia sat silently holding Laurel Stafford's hand. Outside a pickup crunched gravel.

"It's a kind of catatonic stupor," Mia said then. "It doesn't seem to be a neurocognitive condition. From the reports, doctors don't think it's chemical either. This kind of withdrawal has different psychological causes—anxiety, depression, PTSD. For some reason, she just . . . hides. Nothing special brings it on. She's here, and then she isn't."

Laurel Stafford gazed straight ahead. What she saw I couldn't say. But what I saw was something I'd seen before. "Men in combat, sometimes . . ."

"Yes," Mia said.

Newt descended the stairs. He came in and handed me the Glock. The pistol was loaded, on safe. It had been fired, but not recently.

"I'm not much of a Marine, I guess," he said. "I haven't cleaned it."

I handed him the gun. "I think Merle's back. Let's step outside a minute, shall we."

He hesitated. He raised the gun, looked at it as if unsure of its purpose. Then he lowered it to his side.

We went out onto the porch. The pickup was parked beside the Lexus.

"Must be in the shop," Newt said. "He went in for some hardware. He should be coming up here soon."

"I think I'll go down. But . . ."

Again I debated. But not long. Newton Ragatz was a Marine.

I told him quickly what I knew and what I suspected.

We looked out at the desert, empty land drab and winter gray. Like

Laurel Stafford, everything alive in it had gone into hiding. I thought of Paltry, guarding nothing from nothing.

Finally, Newt spoke. "What are you going to do?"

"I don't know," I said. "Talk to him. See what happens."

After another silence, with quiet assurance he said, "He's a Marine."

At that moment the shop door opened. Merle Stafford stepped into the sunlight, looked up, with his hand hailed me, and then disappeared back inside.

I had no plan. I had no clear objective or desired outcome. I had no gun. So I wasn't doing what I didn't do anymore.

I left Newt Ragatz on the porch. The light patch in the corner of the black rectangle of earth was still visible. The shop, when I stepped inside, was warm, smelled of coffee brewing. Merle Stafford handed me an empty cup.

"Have a good chat with Newt?"

"Good enough," I said.

"Laurel okay?"

"They're taking care of her."

He smiled, nearly. "She—the girl, the nurse, she's real good with her. And with Newt."

I'd thought so too. "Something going to come of that, you think?"

"Maybe," he said. "She's spent the night. Slept in the guest room, but still . . . Ain't hard to tell she'd like to get closer to Newt. What he thinks, though, that's always the question."

"Yeah," I said. "Another question is who blew Rollo Kohler's face off the other night."

He went grim. "And you think it was Newt? Goddamn it, Ross, you think, what? That he took that bastard's gun so he could use it on him?"

"I don't think anything, Gunny. Except that whoever did it got to Rollo Kohler before I did. Kept me from murder."

His silence said that he hadn't heard about Alicia.

"My ex-wife was killed in a fire. Arson."

He nodded, coughed. "Sorry."

"Yeah," I said, "me too."

The gurgling of brewing coffee slowed, stopped. Almost wearily he took up the pot and filled two cups, handed me one.

"I've been thinking about guns," I said. "I'd guess you've got one fairly close to hand."

Without answering, he moved to his workbench, slid open the drawer, and retrieved the old .45 Colt. He placed it carefully on the table between us.

"You've had plenty of time to clean it," I said.

He looked at me, waiting.

"At first I thought Newt." I tasted the coffee. "But the Glock hasn't been fired recently. And Paulie Hauberk, one of Len Maglie's troops, carries a cannon, but he didn't do it."

He watched, waited.

"Paulie's the guy who got his hand shot off when Howie and friends robbed Bryce Ragatz twenty-five years ago. He was shot by a .45."

He shifted his shoulders. I thought he was going to pick up the gun, but he didn't. Instead he raised his coffee cup.

I went on. "I'd guess too that Paulie was shot by that particular .45. I don't think it was in your bedside table, Gunny. I think you'd buried it in your barn, and you dug it up the other day. I mean, digging a hole looking for a foundation, that's pretty lame."

He scraped at his throat, finally spoke. "This is just us, huh? Marine to Marine?"

"I'm an officer of the court." I had a duty. I'd sworn an oath. "Don't tell me anything I'll be honor-bound to pass on."

Slowly he shook his head. "No, fuck that. No lawyer games. Just you and me. Then you do what you have to."

So we drank coffee as he talked about killing people.

Rollo Kohler had phoned, insisting that Merle and Laurel Stafford must have killed her husband and taken the money stolen from Bryce Ragatz. Rollo threatened to torch their home if they didn't pay him off. For Merle, enough was enough. He drove to the Kohler house in Sparks and waited for Rollo to return. Then he shot him in the back of the head. He had no regrets.

"You didn't want to break his neck?"

"I wanted to be sure," he said. He coughed. "He was a big fucker, who knows what might have happened in a tussle."

"Okay. And you shot him with a handgun you'd dug up a couple of days before. A weapon that a ballistics check will show had been used in an armed robbery a couple of decades past."

"Yeah," he said quietly, "that's what I did."

"And Joe?"

He didn't feel guilty about Joe Kohler either. He was an asshole, he'd once put his hands on Laurel, and now he was trying to burn and bully money out of them. He was going to make sure that Laurel heard about Howie Ragatz and Gale Dunn. So Merle killed him. He'd felt something like pleasure as he snapped the old man's diseased bones. No regrets.

"How did you feel busting him up with a tire iron after he was dead?"

"Not good," he acknowledged. "But not bad enough to stop."

He did regret killing Gale Dunn. He hadn't planned to, he'd gone to talk to her, to scare her if need be, so that she'd stop plaguing them with ugly phone calls, one of which he was fearful that his wife might somehow answer. But Gale Dunn didn't scare. She was drunk, spewing sewage. She ignored him, wouldn't stop the filth. So he stopped it.

Newt wasn't the only Marine who knew how to snap a neck.

He killed her because, then and there, suddenly it simplified everything, solved the problem. And because he was tired. He wanted everything over.

But almost immediately he understood that he'd crossed a line. He'd violated an oath. He'd dishonored himself.

"I don't believe in much, Ross," he said, "But when it comes down to it, I believe in the Corps. And a Marine wouldn't do what I did."

I drank my coffee. I understood what he'd said. I found that I didn't care about the deaths of Rollo and Joe Kohler. I should have, probably, but I didn't. But like Merle Stafford, I couldn't get past caring about the woman who wanted more. The woman who would not believe that she had been abandoned and betrayed. The angry, awful woman who lived with death in her head.

But I didn't have the whole story.

"Were they right?"

He frowned. "Who?"

"All of them, Gunny. Everybody, at one time or another, thought that you and Laurel must have killed Howie Ragatz."

He warmed up our coffee. As he was pouring, he left the .45 unattended between us. I might have made a move for it. He might have wanted me to. But I just watched him. And waited.

"It was an accident," he said.

Merle Stafford told me, slowly, quietly, what had happened.

The robbery of Bryce Ragatz had been Maglie's idea, but when he was supposed to be meeting Howie in Sun Valley to divide the money, he was having his appendix chopped out. Dick Pym was dead. Joe Kohler, who didn't know Maglie was involved, was in jail. And Howie Ragatz found himself with an attaché case full of cash and a head start of several days.

"Everything just fell into place for him," Merle said. "Who was he to argue against luck like that? He called his girlfriend. He packed a bag. Then his luck ran out."

Merle had driven Laurel and Newt to Park Lane Mall, where they priced refrigerators at Sears and bought Newt clothes at Gottschalks. They returned just as Howie was tossing his bag into the trunk of his car. When Laurel took the boy inside, Howie couldn't resist bragging to Merle about what he'd pulled off. Merle, angry, grabbed and opened the attaché case. Laurel came back outside. Then the woman who so often saw so little saw the money and knew that her husband was leaving her. She flew at him, he shoved her and she fell, and Merle Stafford knocked him down. Howie got up and pulled a gun. Merle wrenched Howie's arm and the gun fell to the ground. Merle picked it up, Howie reached for it, and the gun went off.

I anticipated the rest. "You took the gun and the body and drove out here and buried them in your barn."

He coughed, nodded.

"They still there, the remains of Howie Ragatz?"

"Yes."

"And the money?"

"It too."

That surprised me.

"She didn't want it," he said. Then he corrected himself. "She didn't want to spend it. She just wanted to know it was there if she—we—needed it. I saw to it that we didn't."

I drained my coffee cup. "Well, it's a nice story, Gunny. Some of it's probably true. That stuff about how the gun went off is pure bullshit, though, isn't it?"

He looked at me.

"If it were the truth, you could have just called the sheriff. I mean, you've got the gun, you've got the money, you've got an alibi for the robbery—the law is going to give you a hard time, but finally they're going to accept that it happened just the way you said."

He didn't respond.

"Except you've got a problem. Fingerprints. You can't wipe the pistol clean, that would give the game away. And you can't explain how hers come to be there."

He spoke then. "Fuck you, Ross."

He cleared his throat, and I heard, finally, what he had been hiding from me. "Tell me again about this cough, Gunny."

He looked at me but said nothing.

"I should have picked up on it," I said. "You're a man setting his affairs in order."

He looked at the pistol. He looked at me. "What are you going to do?"

I shrugged. "I'm going to try to comfort my grieving daughter."

Now he did pick up the .45, waving it slowly. "But about all this?"

I rose. “It’s none of my business, Gunny.”

He looked like an old man, small, hopeless, dying.

I went to the door, opened it to the cold, turned back. He waited for me to say something. Much as I might want to, I could offer him no comfort, no consolation. There was only one thing a man like me could say to a man like him.

“Semper Fi.”

ACKNOWLEDGMENTS

I wish to thank Christine Kelly and her editorial staff—Margaret Dalrymple, Wes Reid, and Danilo John Thomas—for all their help in preparing this novel for publication. Thanks as well to the friends who read and commented on the manuscript: Bill Baines, Michael Binard, Kathy Boardman, Phil Boardman, Mike Croft, Ray Embry, Barb Gilbert, Danny Goeschl, Robert Merrill, Gaye Nichols, John Pettey, and Ann Schopen.

About the Author

Bernard Schopen was born and raised in Deadwood, South Dakota. After an enlistment in the United States Navy, he attended Black Hills State College, the University of Washington, and the University of Nevada-Reno. For many years he taught English and Humanities, first at Truckee Meadows Community College, then at St. Anselm's College, and finally at the University of Nevada, Reno. He is the author of four Jack Ross mysteries, as well as two other novels, *Calamity Jane* and *The Last Centurion*, both published by Baobab Press. In 2000, he was inducted into the Nevada Writers Hall of Fame.

The body of The Dying Time is set in Times New Roman, a serif typeface designed for legibility in body text. It was commissioned by the British newspaper *The Times* in 1931 and conceived by Stanley Morison, the artistic advisor to the British branch of the printing equipment company Monotype, in collaboration with Victor Lardent, a lettering artist in *The Times'* advertising department.

The cover and headers are set in Baskerville URW. Baskerville is a serif typeface designed in the 1750s by John Baskerville (1706–1775) in Birmingham, England, and cut into metal by punchcutter John Handy. Baskerville is classified as a transitional typeface. Compared to earlier designs popular in Britain, Baskerville increased the contrast between thick and thin strokes, making the serifs sharper and more tapered, and shifted the axis of rounded letters to a more vertical position .

CPSIA information can be obtained
at www.ICGtesting.com
Printed in the USA
LVHW021943110119
603646LV00005B/5/P